Cecily von Ziegesa...

a priv...e girls' sch...

...ter,

and sh...

...2 DEC...

...OSSIP G...

...els

were inevit...

Created by Cecily von Ziegesar

Gossip Girl
the Carlyles

you just can't get enough

Created by

Cecily von Ziegesar

Written by

Annabelle Vestry

<u>headline</u>

Produced by Alloy Entertainment
151 West 26th Street, New York, NY 10001, USA

First published in Great Britain in 2008 by
HEADLINE PUBLISHING GROUP

1

Cataloguing in Publication Data is available from the British Library

ISBN 978 0 7553 3986 0

Typeset in Plantin by Palimpsest Book Production Limited, Grangemouth, Stirlingshire

Printed in the UK by CPI Mackays, Chatham, ME5 8TD

Headline's policy is to use papers that are natural, renewable and recyclable products and made from wood grown in sustainable forests. The logging and manufacturing processes are expected to conform to the environmental regulations of the country of origin.

HEADLINE PUBLISHING GROUP
An Hachette Livre UK Company
338 Euston Road
London NW1 3BH

www.headline.co.uk
www.hachettelivre.co.uk

It is better to be feared than loved, if you cannot be both.

Niccolò Machiavelli

gossipgirl.net

Disclaimer: All the real names of places, people, and events have been altered or abbreviated to protect the innocent. Namely, me.

| topics | sightings | your e-mail | post a question |

hey people!

a new era

News flash: This year's juniors are the people to watch. Seniors and college applications? Who cares? Who wants to waste time on boring will-they-or-won't-they-get-in speculation when there's so much partying without consequences going on? Now that our Alice + Olivia frocks are tucked away and it's getting darker earlier, it's time to really get down to business. There are benefits to host, hearts to break, relationships to consummate, facial hair to shave (yes, I'm specifically addressing a certain swim team here), and a whole city to play in. So go out there and shake things up. Talk to that cutie in the Riverside Prep cap. Forge new friendships. Maybe even some rivalries. Throw a wild party, and just as it's heating up, make it *wilder*. And who better to emulate than the newbies taking NYC by storm?

The NKOTB

The Carlyle triplets certainly know how to have fun. We've got **A**, blond, blue-eyed, and innocent on the outside. Who would have guessed she has a knack for throwing crazy parties – so crazy that she wound up behind bars? Luckily, she's already won the hearts of the whole junior class, as well as of the board of overseers at Constance Billard. Talk about a people person. And then there's six-foot-two, Adonis-like, Speedo-clad **O**. He's surprisingly still single, despite the bevy of available girls following him everywhere, from swim practice to Red Bull runs at Duane Reade. Is he holding out for a certain someone? And does anyone know who that certain someone could be? Finally, there's our little **B**, who seems to have shifted her allegiance from one tiny sandy eastern seaboard island to *our* little island. Can you blame her? Especially when she has golden boy **J.P.** as a tour guide? But after breaking the rules at Constance and being asked to take a much-buzzed-about week of 'garden leave' (aka private-school suspension), will she be allowed to stay? Or will her unconventionality prove too much for 10021?

sightings

J at scholarship auditions for the School of American Ballet. Great tours jetés, but is that enough? **R** having afternoon tea with his mom, **Lady S**, at Soho House. **A** going to a waxing appointment at Elizabeth Arden Red Door Salon with **S.J.**, **G**, and the rest of **J**'s posse. Is this how we bond now? Waxing together? And mysteriously absent from the happy crew? **J** herself. Why bail on a waxing trip? Has someone gone all European on us? **O** running solo, up Hudson River Park. He really should stretch afterward. I can help!

your e-mail

Dear GG,

So, I sort of extended this South American trip and missed the first two weeks of school, and now everything is freaking crazy! Are **B** and **J.P.** really together? And what about **J**? Is she with anyone? What's happening to our world?

– Existential Freakout

Dear E.F.,

Extending a trip into the school year is so last year. Anyway, to get you up to speed, **B** and **J.P.** got to know each other when, lover (of animals!) that **B** is, she volunteered to walk **J.P.**'s dogs. Now the dogwalker is back from her whirlwind marriage and honeymoon to her employer's gardener, so **B** is out of a job, but she and **J.P.** are still hanging out. We'll see how long they can keep their paws . . . uh, hands, off each other. As for **J**, she's alone . . . for now. But don't cry for her, Argentina (or wherever you trekked off to), because she can take care of herself.

– GG

Dear Gossip Girl,

I've never written on this site before, but I'm a paralegal working on a very important historic property, and I'm absolutely appalled that, during a party there last week, a very valuable copy of *The Collected Works of William Shakespeare* was stolen. If you have any information at all on how this could have transpired, I would be grateful.

– LawandOrder

Dear L&O,

Doesn't Shakespeare speak the language of love? Maybe someone took it to get ideas. Start with the bachelors and work your way from there.

– GG

And that's a wrap! I'm going to soak up the last days of summer with a glass of sparkling wine at the roof garden at the Met. Yes, it's old school, but with so much action taking place on the museum steps or in Central Park, how can I resist?

You know you love me,

sealed with a kiss . . .

'Do you think I should give Mrs McLean the sculpture?' Edie Carlyle gestured to the bulky, misshapen bag slung over her shoulder.

Baby Carlyle peered dubiously into the hemp bag. A bubble gum pink bowl was nestled inside, undoubtedly one of her mother's latest art projects. An MTA city bus roared by, causing Baby's green linen dress, purchased from a cart near Central Park for ten dollars, to billow around her skinny knees. Baby shrugged.

'Well, I don't want you to get kicked out,' Edie fretted as they crossed East Ninety-third Street toward the Constance Billard School for Girls.

Baby was technically still enrolled in the small, elite, uniform-required institution that her mother had also attended years ago. But after skipping several mandatory after-school service hours for minor French class infractions, she'd been placed on 'garden leave' for a week. It turned out 'garden leave' was just a fancy private school term for suspension. For the past week, she had spent her days drinking chai on a bench in Central Park, reading Nabokov, and waiting for her new friend J. P. Cashman to get out of school at Riverside Prep. Then they'd spend the afternoon in Central Park, playing with his three dogs, reading books to each other, and having long, rambling conversations about their childhoods. Now, though, Baby bit her cherry-ChapSticked lower lip nervously. What if she actually got expelled?

A week ago, that was *all* she had wanted. While her brother, Owen, and sister, Avery, had seemed to feel at home as soon as they set foot in Manhattan, Baby, the smallest and most independent Carlyle triplet, had just felt . . . lost. She'd been overwhelmed with homesickness for their ramshackle house back in Siasconset, Nantucket, and her boyfriend, Tom Devlin. So she'd done what had seemed like the logical thing at the time: intentionally gotten herself into trouble at school, hoping her mom would realize how unfit she was for Constance and New York. But when she surprised Tom by showing up back in Nantucket, and realized that he was not only a raging stoner but a raging *cheater*, she began to reconsider New York City. Especially after J.P., a boy Baby had written off as a typical spoiled Upper East Sider, flew up to Nantucket in his father's helicopter to ask her to come back to Manhattan.

Beats a text message.

Baby sighed and pushed her long, wavy brunette bangs off her high forehead. If she did get kicked out, she didn't know what she'd do. Surely none of the other schools in Manhattan would take her, except maybe Darrow, a small school down in the Village where all the students, from kindergartners to seniors, were taught in the same classroom. She wrinkled her nose, imagining finger painting with five-year-olds while listening to Joni Mitchell songs. She was bohemian, but not *that* bohemian.

And we're all very thankful for that.

Edie banged open Constance Billard's royal blue doors, the silver energy chakra–balancing pendants dangling from her neck clinking against one another.

'Wait.' Edie held the door open for her daughter as she deftly moved the hemp bag from one skinny arm to another. She took off one of her large, ugly, blob-shaped necklaces. 'Wear this for luck,' she commanded, her blue eyes flashing.

Baby offered a small smile and clasped the pendant around her neck. It looked like an amoeba, multiplied a million times under a microscope.

'It's this way,' Baby mumbled, guiding her mom down Constance's polished, empty halls. They were eerily quiet, since everyone was in their last-period classes.

Edie followed, her unfashionable Birkenstocks thwacking against the freshly buffed marble floors of the school. They paused at a heavy oak door with HEADMISTRESS written on it in intimidating gold block letters.

'I remember this place.' Edie ruffled her daughter's already tangled brown hair. 'I spent enough time here myself when I was a student.'

Baby nodded. It was hard to imagine her bohemian mom wearing the stiff, knee-length seersucker skirts that were part of the mandatory Constance uniform, even as a teenager. Baby glanced at a plaque on the wall, engraved with the names of past class presidents. Her sister, Avery, would kill to get on that plaque. Baby was just glad there wasn't a plaque for Constance delinquents. She was sure her name would top that list.

Unless, of course, her mom already held that honor.

'Baby Carlyle?' The stringy-haired secretary looked up, her eyes disapproving slits as she gave Baby a quick once-over. Baby nodded and smiled thinly. Her heart thumped against her chest.

'Go right in – Mrs McLean is expecting you.' The secretary blinked her eyes and then looked back at her computer. She began typing furiously, undoubtedly sending an all-points bulletin to the rest of the faculty that French class–interrupting, school service–hour skipping, Mason Pearson hairbrush–boycotting Baby Carlyle was back.

Judgment day!

'Ah, thank you for coming.' Mrs McLean stood up from behind her large oak desk as Baby and Edie shuffled inside. She wore a black pantsuit that was two sizes too small. One button midway down the jacket was hanging on to the material by a thread, like a baby koala clinging to a eucalyptus tree.

'Sit,' she commanded as she practically pushed Baby down onto a dark blue love seat. The velvet fabric was stiff and scratched the back of Baby's bare legs.

'Mrs McLean, I'm Baby's mother, Edie.' Her mom grabbed the headmistress's hand and pumped it vigorously. 'So nice of you to take this time to meet with us. Here – I made this for you,' Edie announced as she rooted through her hemp bag. She pulled out the misshapen bubble gum pink bowl and plunked it upside down on Mrs McLean's desk. It had a small nub in the center.

Surprise registered in Mrs McLean's large, freckled face. She was probably used to mothers with kids in trouble plunking down checks, not homemade, lumpy pottery. 'Thank you for . . . that, Mrs Carlyle.'

'Oh, call me Edie! But I see it doesn't go with the décor,' Edie realized sadly, shifting her gaze from the sculpture to the office's red, white, and blue furnishings.

'Um, that's quite all right.' Mrs McLean settled back into her oak chair. 'Let's begin. Now, I know *Baby* . . .' Mrs McLean paused, a sour expression on her Raggedy-Ann face. In a school populated by girls with names like Beatrice and Madison, the headmistress had made it clear she didn't find Baby's name completely appropriate. But it wasn't *Baby's* fault her mother had thought she was only having twins, and had just stuck the name Baby on her birth certificate. According to the story, Edie had always meant to give Baby a more formal name, but, in her anything-goes tradition, she'd simply never gotten around to it. Because she was the baby of the family, and of such diminutive stature, the name had naturally stuck.

'I know Baby had, ahem, an *unconventional* upbringing,' Mrs McLean continued. 'Which most likely contributed to her difficult transition at Constance her first week of school. During her time off, my hope was that Baby would take the week to reflect on her behavior while we came to a conclusion about her future, and whether or not her future included Constance Billard.' Mrs McLean carefully pushed the lumpy bowl to the edge of her desk. The headmistress had a splotch of maroon-colored lipstick on her front teeth, and all of a sudden Baby felt a tug of sympathy for her. Maybe she felt as out of place at Constance as Baby did. 'So, Baby, did you find your week off productive?'

'I did,' Baby replied, glancing around the office. She wasn't sure why she wanted to stay at Constance so badly, but for the past week it had been all she could think about. As much as she missed Nantucket and all its shoreside beauty, that was all in the past. New York was her home now.

Wonder what – or *who* – changed her mind?

'Ma'am,' Baby added, then blushed. Next thing she knew, she'd be curtsying.

Or saluting. Yes, sir, Mrs McLean, sir!

'Well, I've looked through your transcript, and I've reached a decision.' Mrs McLean crossed her arms over her voluminous chest.

Baby wasn't looking forward to begging her way back into the world of bitchy girls with Oscar Blandi-highlighted hair, Gucci ponytail holders, and Montblanc pens. But she was ready to do it. She licked her lips and locked her dark eyes with Mrs McLean's muddy brown ones. 'Mrs—'

'Baby will be permitted to stay at Constance,' the headmistress interrupted.

Baby breathed a sigh of relief.

'But to prove to me that adjusting to Constance's strict codes of conduct will be possible for her, she will need to do Constance community service,' Mrs McLean continued. 'In earnest this time. Since she comes from such an, ahem, artistic background, I have what I believe to be an appropriate task for her . . .' Mrs McLean bent down, her voluminous behind swaying in the air as she rifled through a shiny metal cabinet. When she stood up, she handed Baby a black-and-white magazine with a photo of a dead pigeon on the front. *Rancor* was written across the front in angry-looking capital letters.

'This is our student-run art magazine. Its creator and editor graduated last year.' Mrs McLean squinted her cowlike eyes. '*Rancor* requires an artistic sensibility, and I'm hoping you'll be willing to take it on,' she finished. Edie clapped her hands excitedly, as if Mrs McLean had designed the task for her and not her daughter.

Baby took the magazine and flipped through its pages. Despite the edgy cover, the inside was full of cheesy poems about ice-skating in Rockefeller Center and the smell of flowers in spring. Baby tried to imagine working on the magazine but couldn't. Unlike her spirited sister, who was currently the student liaison to the board of overseers at Constance, school spirit had never really been her thing.

'Well, I am so glad that this is all straightened out, and of course Baby is grateful for the opportunity,' Edie said abruptly. 'But now I have to go – I absolutely *must* get back to my studio.' She swooped down and planted a kiss on the top of Baby's head. Baby could smell her mother's patchouli-infused essential-oil scent. She grinned to herself, careful that Mrs McLean didn't see her smirking. Her mother's randomness was so over-the-top that it could seem almost like an act.

'Of course.' Mrs McLean nodded, as if she understood the pressing nature of Edie's art. 'Baby, we'll see you tomorrow, bright and early. And I don't need to remind you that you need to be in uniform,' she added.

'Yes, of course! Thank you, Mrs McLean,' Baby said gratefully. She grinned and kept on grinning as she left the office and scampered out the school's royal blue doors. She leaned against the redbrick building to collect herself, knowing she only had a moment before the bell would ring and girls would come pouring out in droves. Even though she wasn't thrilled about revamping some neglected student magazine, she couldn't help but feel like she'd dodged a bullet. Yes, Constance was a little uptight and full of prissy girls, but Baby's life had felt unstable ever since she'd been uprooted from Nantucket, and now it felt like things were getting back on track.

'Hey there!'

Baby whirled around to see J.P., clad in khakis and his blue Riverside Prep blazer, standing at the corner. He was holding a rainbow sno-cone in one hand, his BlackBerry in the other.

Baby loved how J.P. seemed so buttoned-up but wasn't really. Not when you got to know him. And now that she was officially here to stay on the Upper East Side, she intended to get to know him a whole lot better.

As in, know him in the biblical sense?

'Celebratory sno-cone? Did everything go okay with your meeting?' J.P. pushed his floppy brown hair from his eyes nervously.

'I'm not going anywhere,' Baby said triumphantly. 'You can tell the dogs not to worry,' she teased.

'Good.' J.P. grinned. 'I wouldn't want them to lapse into their bad habits without you.' Baby instinctively looked down at J.P.'s feet. Before she'd started walking his dogs, Nemo had had an attitude problem and had taken to pooping on J.P.'s shoes. Today J.P. wore soft leather moccasins that looked like they'd been stolen from a Native American exhibit at the Museum of Natural History, but Baby knew they'd been picked out by a personal shopper at Barneys – all of J.P.'s clothes were.

Rule of thumb: the uglier a boy's shoes, the more expensive they are.

Baby grabbed the sno-cone and licked it, enjoying the rush of cold and sugar on her tongue. She felt giddy and relieved. She wasn't sure what was making her happier: that she was staying at Constance, or that J.P. cared enough about her fate to leave school early and surprise her.

Just then, the bell rang, and hordes of uniform-wearing,

shiny-haired girls came streaming out the royal blue doors. They moved toward the sidewalk or stood in clusters on the school's steps, gossiping about their days. A few stared at Baby and J.P., whispering behind their Bliss-manicured hands.

Baby spotted Jack Laurent, J.P.'s bitchtastic ballerina ex-girlfriend, exiting the double doors. She stopped walking when her green eyes landed on Baby, her back ramrod straight. With her lightly freckled nose held high and her glossy, pin-straight auburn hair, she looked like she belonged on the catwalk rather than the steps of Constance Billard.

Baby shrugged and turned her back to Jack, facing J.P. instead. Who even cared about Jack Laurent? All that mattered was that she'd spent the past week hanging out with an adorable boy who got more adorable every day. And she intended to spend the next year doing the same thing.

Impulsively Baby leaned into J.P. and planted her lips on his. His eyes widened in surprise, but he eagerly kissed her back. Baby wrapped her thin arms around him. His lips tasted like eucalyptus. She felt a shiver go up and down her spine and settle into her stomach as she kissed him again. His arms felt strong around her, and his mouth tasted so clean and uncomplicated.

'Thanks for the sno-cone,' Baby whispered as she finally drew back, still in J.P.'s arms. She felt another shiver run down her spine. Wow. Why hadn't she done that sooner?

'Let's get out of here,' J.P. whispered huskily, pulling her down the school's steps. Baby took his hand, her hip bumping against his as they walked west toward the goldfish-colored sun and the lush greenery of Central Park.

Maybe it's time to trade in the tie-dye for an I LOVE NEW YORK tee?

j is for jealousy

Jack Laurent gripped the metal railing of the Constance steps with her petal pink fingernails, feeling like she'd been slapped. No, *slapped* wasn't the right word. She felt like she'd been pushed off a high dive into an empty concrete pool. The kiss she'd just witnessed replayed on a loop in her mind. She could not *believe* that bohemian hippie slut had just kissed her boyfriend.

Doesn't she mean *ex*-boyfriend?

Jack tried to regain her composure. She focused on breathing in and out, ignoring the Constance girls streaming past her. *Perfect, perfect, perfect,* she chanted in her head. In the past, the word had always helped her get composed. But lately, it hadn't been working so well. She couldn't tune out the whispers of the eighth graders bounding down the steps.

'I heard the reason Baby Carlyle was gone this week was to walk, like, all the shows at fashion week. Apparently, there's this whole hippie revival that Marc Jacobs is doing, starring her,' one wiry blond eighth grader whispered to her unfortunately turnip-shaped friend as they clattered down the steps.

Jack glared at them with her catlike green eyes, trying

not to freak the fuck out. She felt like Blanche DuBois in *A Streetcar Named Desire*, right before she gets carted off to a mental hospital.

She checked her watch impatiently. Where the *fuck* were her friends? And what could J.P. Cashman, her mogul-in-training ex-boyfriend, *possibly* have in common with a girl from *nowhere*, Nantucket, who looked like she was just waiting for Woodstock 3? It was absurd.

But the trouble was, everything in Jack's life was absurd lately. Ever since her wealthy former French ambassador father had cut her and her mother off from his black AmEx – and forced them to move into the musty garret above what had been their Upper East Side town house – nothing in Jack's life had gone according to plan. A picture-perfect family, including a five-year-old girl named Satchel, had moved into the house below. From her bedroom, Jack could hear the family having cocktail parties, laughing, and clinking their silver, which made her feel like the crazy lady in *Jane Eyre*, relegated to the attic. It was all too depressing. When she'd begged her father to reconsider, all she'd gotten was a lecture about responsibility. Until Jack could prove that she wouldn't end up a chain-smoking, histrionic shopaholic like her overly dramatic French mother, Charles Laurent wasn't going to finance *anything* except school.

Whatever. Jack had already sucked it up and nailed her School of American Ballet scholarship audition over the weekend, and she had just bought the most adorable kitten-heel Miu Mius with one of the Barneys gift cards she'd found stuck in her Hermès wallet, left over from her sixteenth birthday. She looked down and smiled at how cute the shoes looked at the ends of her bare, ballet-toned legs. The ten-dollar pedi place on Third actually wasn't as gross and dirty as she'd thought it would be. So her father wanted to play games? She'd become fabulously successful and make her own money. Then she'd write a tell-all memoir, set up a dance camp for less privileged girls like herself, and appear on *Oprah*. The famous talk show host wouldn't be able to help but cry when she heard Jack's story, and her father would start throwing money at her.

Sounds like a plan!

Jack sighed impatiently and pulled her long auburn hair over her shoulder, examining the ends. She could definitely use a trim from Raoul, her favorite stylist at the John Barrett Salon, but, sadly, that was out of the question. She pulled her hair back into a sleek bun, securing it with a Sephora barrette. She *hated* waiting. The free time just made her start obsessing over everything. Like, for instance, why the fuck did her friends think it was okay to keep her waiting? She pulled out a pack of Merits from her large, rust-colored Givenchy satchel, a constant reminder of the girl she once was and the things she'd formerly taken for granted. She lit up with her Tiffany engraved lighter, not caring that smoking on school property was technically grounds for disciplinary action. After all, their lesbo headmistress, Mrs McLean, had apparently let Baby back in after she'd practically been *expelled*. Jack doubted she'd get in trouble for something so minor as smoking.

'You're allowed to smoke here?'

Jack heard an annoyingly perky voice behind her. She turned around to see none other than Avery Carlyle, who sounded like she was really fucking *curious* about Constance's rules.

'Hey Avery,' Jack replied fake-sweetly, wishing she could blow smoke in Avery's face. Avery was the only person at

Constance who knew about Jack's financial situation, and, as such, pretty much owned Jack. Jack had tried to destroy Avery and her bid for the student liaison for the board of overseers position by secretly calling the cops at the out-of-control party Avery had hosted at her grandmother's town house a week ago. Instead, when the cops had broken up Avery's party – *arresting* the hostess – everyone had treated her like a rock star, and she'd even won the board of overseers position. Not like Jack had really wanted it anyway. But it hurt not to have been elected by her class-mates, and it would have made her dad a little more likely to open up his checkbook for her.

'Hey.' Avery smiled, pushing her thick, blond, split-end-free hair back under an extra-wide black leather Coach headband. It made her look like Alice in fucking Wonderland.

Jack stared in disbelief as Sarah Jane Jenson, Jiffy Bennett, and Genevieve Coursy – *her* friends – emerged from the building and immediately circled around Avery like tourists around an umbrella-toting Fifth Avenue tour guide on a rainy day. Jack glared. For the past week, her friends had included Avery in everything they did, and while Jack was by no means out, Avery was certainly *in*.

'So, Stella McCartney's having a sample sale downtown. Want to go?' Avery stepped back to let Jack into the circle and cocked her head expectantly.

'We're going.' Genevieve shrugged as she thrust her hand in Jack's purse, pulling the pack of Merits from its depths and taking out a cigarette.

'Want one?' She offered the pack to Avery, hardly acknowledging Jack.

Avery shook her head primly and smiled. 'No thanks,

I don't smoke. Are you coming?' Avery asked Jack expect-antly. Her blue eyes were wide open and friendly, making Jack feel like the extreme bitch that she was. It was as if Avery was this new and improved friend to Genevieve, Jiffy, and Sarah Jane, all freshly scrubbed and idealistic.

And carcinogen-free?

Jack again fought the urge to blow smoke all over Avery's self-righteous face. After all, Avery hadn't been that inno-cent at her party. After being hauled to the police station, she'd been thrown in the drunk tank until her brother, Owen, came to rescue her. Jack mutinously grabbed the pack of Merits out of Genevieve's hands and stuffed it back into her bag. Just two weeks ago, they had all been talking about what a loser Avery Carlyle was.

'Fine, I'll go.' Jack shrugged and sighed deeply, as if going to a sample sale was a huge sacrifice. It wasn't like she could fucking afford it, but she didn't want to leave Avery with her friends unattended.

'Great.' Avery smiled and put her hand out to hail a cab. Immediately, one screeched to the curb. Avery opened the door as the rest of the girls crammed in next to her, giggling. It was a regular-size cab where *really* only three people could fit in the back, but no cabbie would say no to five cute, uniformed private-school girls who were willing to sit on one another's laps.

Jack sighed and stalked to the front seat of the cab. It was the ultimate humiliation to sit in the passenger seat, next to the cab driver, as if they were pals or some-thing. Jack thought wistfully back to the days when she'd had a sleek black Lincoln Town Car at her disposal to take her from ballet classes to school. It all seemed so long ago.

Just then, Avery's phone erupted into the first few notes of 'Material Girl.' Old-school '80s Madonna? Was she serious? Jack wrinkled her nose and turned around to roll her eyes at Genevieve, but she was texting furiously on her Treo while Jiffy and Sarah Jane looked over her shoulder. No one had even *asked* Jack how her day was.

Avery pulled her phone out of her purse and looked at the display. She didn't recognize the number, which was actually sort of exciting. She was getting calls from people she didn't even know! After a shaky first week, all of a sudden it felt like *everyone* wanted to hang out with her. She was on a constant high, as though champagne bubbles were coursing through her veins. Avery flipped open her phone and answered excitedly. 'Hello?'

'Avery Carlyle?' An unfamiliar, wavery, old-lady voice was on the other end of the line.

'Yes?' Avery replied suspiciously.

'Muffy St Clair.'

Avery racked her brain, then remembered the kindly old woman who had announced her student liaison to the board of overseers win at the Constance mother-daughter brunch at Tavern on the Green. Avery sat up straighter and smoothed an invisible wrinkle from her Constance uniform.

'Yes, how are you, Muffy?' Avery asked in her sweetest, most professional voice. Jiffy giggled when she heard the name Muffy. *Jiffy* of all people shouldn't laugh, Avery sniffed. Muffy was an old-fashioned and New York–y name. She shot Jiffy a disapproving look and turned her full attention back to the phone. This was important!

'We're having a meeting at the Pierre to discuss Constance. You can make it? Tomorrow at four,' Muffy boomed into the phone. Avery had to pull it away from her ear. Muffy was obviously of the generation of women who didn't trust cell phones and thought she had to speak extra loud to be heard. Her grandmother had been the same way. If Avery rolled down the cab window, she could probably *hear* Muffy bellowing down Fifth Avenue.

'Sure!' Avery squeaked. 'Can't wait!' She hung up quickly. 'Constance stuff.' She shrugged apologetically to the girls.

'Fun.' Sarah Jane rolled her eyes and pulled out a copy of *Tatler* magazine from her bag. Sarah Jane's mom was the editor in chief of *Bella*, a major fashion magazine, and Sarah Jane, determined to follow in her mother's patent-leather Manolo footsteps, was always reading British magazines and complaining about American media.

Avery leaned back happily, even though they kept lurching and stopping in the midday Fifth Avenue traffic and she usually got sort of carsick in cabs. She heard Jack sigh in the front seat and realized she'd been pretty quiet lately. Maybe it was because of her ex-boyfriend? It *was* kind of weird that Baby and he were hanging out so much. She wondered how much Jack knew about them.

Too much.

Avery reached through the plastic divider window that separated the backseat of the cab from the front and tapped Jack's shoulder with her finger.

'Are you okay?' Avery whispered as she leaned her head partway through the Plexiglas partition. The cab smelled like incense and the driver looked annoyed. Five private school girls might look cute, but they weren't exactly quiet.

Would you have it any other way?

'Perfect,' Jack replied crisply. The cab was stalled in late-afternoon traffic outside the Met. She stared out the window at the throngs of people sitting on the steps. All she could think about were J.P.'s lips on Baby's smart-ass mouth. Suddenly, the overwhelming scent of incense in the cab made her want to throw up.

'Actually, I have to get going,' she said, not explaining any further. She hopped out of the cab, just as the light turned green.

'You're crazy!' the cab driver yelled after her, laying on the horn. Jack shrugged and hobbled over to the steps of the Met. Her shoes might have looked good, but they were a size too small and killing her feet. Fuck. *Fuckity fuck fuck*, she whispered under her breath. Then she remembered, *Perfect*.

'I can take your picture, no?' A Eurotrashy dude in a lime green button-down shirt and tight black pants approached her. He looked like he had hopped straight off one of those ugly red double-decker tourist buses.

'No.' Jack regarded him warily. He was probably just fucking up his sentence construction and wanted *her* to take a picture of *him*, posing cheesily on the steps of the Met. No thank you. She had more important things to do.

Like suck down Merits and feel sorry for herself?

'But you are a model, no? So beautiful! Please give me permission to take a picture?' He bent down on one knee, visibly begging.

Well, that was another thing. Jack nodded regally and squared her shoulders, her chin held up high, posing for the camera. So maybe J.P. didn't want to kiss her anymore, and maybe Avery Carlyle had stolen her friends, her classmates, and pretty much her life. But she was still young and beautiful, and at least *someone* had the good sense to appreciate her.

Ah, how the mighty have fallen.

locking it in in the locker room

Monday after school Rhys Sterling caught sight of himself in the fogged-up mirror in the locker room at the Ninety-second Street Y. He touched his almost-full blackish beard. It obscured his normally angular jawline and made him look sort of like Johnny Depp from *Pirates of the Caribbean*.

Emphasis: sort of.

Rhys sighed angrily as he knotted a royal blue towel neatly around his slim hips. He wished he could just go back to two weeks ago, right before school started, when he was dating Kelsey Talmadge, was hands down the best swimmer on the St Jude's team, and had pretty much everything he ever wanted. Kelsey and he had known each other since kindergarten, and had been dating since the beginning of ninth grade. Everything about her – her puppyish enthusiasm for anything from a street-cart coffee to an opening night at the Met, her utter lack of pretension, even her apple-scented shampoo – made Rhys's life a little bigger, a little brighter, a little *better*. They had spent the summer apart, but Rhys had thought they'd spend the fall reconnecting, and had even planned an ultra-romantic evening for them to lose their virginity to each other. Things hadn't quite gone according to plan.

Oh, that's an understatement.

On the first day of school, Kelsey had broken up with him, telling him there was someone else. To make Rhys feel better, the swim team guys had all taken a vow of chastity, promising not to shave or hook up with a girl until Rhys got some action first. Which seemed like never, especially with his new *Into the Wild* look.

Hey, some girls like a walk on the wild side.

'Lookin' good, man!'

Rhys whirled away from the mirror and glared at Hugh Moore, a muscle-y junior. Hugh pushed his wet golden brown hair out of his eyes. 'So, when's it gonna happen? Maybe you could just borrow one of the ladies who's been following Owen around. He's like a fucking chinchilla or whatever those whacked-out animals are that just follow each other off a cliff, you know, man?' Hugh took a long swig of pink Gatorade and let out a large burp, looking pleased with himself as the sound echoed off the mildew-covered walls.

'Lemmings, not chinchillas,' Rhys muttered as he walked to a row of dented metal lockers. On the other side of the locker room three juniors had pinned down Chadwick Jenkins, a terrified freshman, and were rubbing some type of thick, brownish goo onto his chest from a large green tub.

'It's hair food, man! Dude, if this doesn't make *any* chest hair grow, we'll just know you're a chick,' one of the guys said as he slapped more of the cream onto Chadwick's skinny body.

Rhys wordlessly opened his locker and pulled on a sweatshirt and track pants, barely nodding at Owen Carlyle, who was farther down the row. Weirdly, Owen had seemed just as depressed and quiet as Rhys lately. Rhys couldn't imagine what his problem was. The guy had girls tripping over themselves just to talk to him. Even today, a contingent of L'École girls had spent the entire practice on the observation deck of the pool, giggling every time Owen did a flip turn. Meanwhile, Rhys was surrounded by St Jude's swimmers like Hugh, who were just loud and gross and hairy and . . . *not Kelsey*.

'Hey guys!' Coach Siegel strode into the locker room and blew his metal whistle authoritatively. He stood in the center of the room, his hairless arms crossed over his white STANFORD SWIMMING T-shirt as if he were posing for a *GQ* spread.

'Trying to make Chadwick's hair grow, huh? Reminds me of some of the hazing for the Cardinals!' Coach had graduated from Stanford just a few years ago and talked about it at every opportunity. His mouthwash-blue eyes clouded over in happy reminiscence. 'Come into my office once you're decent, men,' he said, and clapped loudly.

The swimmers crammed into the moist makeshift office. It smelled like BO, feet, and chlorine, mixed with the pungent smell of Polo Double Black – Coach's signature scent. He doused himself with it before he left practice to hit up happy hours. Coach was a notorious player, and the only thing he enjoyed more than telling his swimmers about his conquests was hearing about their own and offering misguided advice.

'It's that time of year.' Coach rubbed his hands together gleefully. 'The St Jude's swim team fund-raiser and date auction. Everyone's being auctioned off, so I hope you all get your girlfriends to show you just how much they love you.' He leered at the row of hairy faces surrounding him. 'So, which of you guys have ladies? Anyone single here?'

Rhys's stomach did a nosedive. He looked around, wondering if he could sneak through the emergency exit door without anyone noticing. He had totally forgotten about the date auction, which happened every year. Technically, the auction was to raise money for some public school's practice time at the Y, but in reality it was just a big private school mixer, an excuse for slutty L'École girls to hook up with St Jude's guys and for parents to gossip about themselves and their perfect children.

See? Benefits benefit *everyone*!

Since he'd been dating Kelsey freshman year, Rhys always had a guaranteed bidder. It had always been so sweet to watch Kelsey shyly raise the paddle for him, whereas the single guys were sometimes left standing like cattle – albeit in crisp Armani tuxes.

'Come on, guys. The bachelors are always the surprise element,' Coach pressed, clearly wishing *he* could be auctioned off as well.

'I'm single!' Chadwick leaped off the floor and raised his scrawny arm. Even covered with the hair-food goo, he probably didn't top a hundred pounds.

'Oh-kay.' Coach looked upward, as if to ask for divine assistance. 'And that'll net a dollar. From your mom,' he cackled, looking hopefully to the team to join in on the joke. Rhys stiffened, a horrible image in his head. What if *his* mom was the only person to bid on him this year? Lady Sterling was the host of the wildly popular afternoon talk show *Tea with Lady Sterling*, a sort of mishmash of manners, etiquette, and society gossip. With his luck, she'd probably tape the whole auction for her show.

'Who else?' Coach surveyed the guys, ranging from linebacker-size Ken Williams to the hobbit-size Ian McDaniel, and grimaced. 'Do we have any other single guys? Come on, gentlemen, I know you spend Friday nights playing with yourselves. This is your chance,' he wheedled.

'Rhys,' Hugh Moore whooped. 'He *needs* a lady. Trust me.'

Coach's eyes lit up. 'Rhys Sterling is single? Okay, Rhys, you're gonna bring in the bucks and get the ladies. I'm telling you, I'm jealous.' Coach winked. 'And, Carlyle? Any ladies in your life?'

'No.' Owen sighed. *Fortunately*, he thought. For the first time in his life, Owen Carlyle was staying away from females. He had met a girl at an out-of-control Nantucket party over the summer, before he'd moved to New York. They'd shared a passionate evening that had culminated in them losing their virginity to each other on the beach. They hadn't even told each other their names, which hadn't seemed trashy at all. Really.

Really?

Instead, it had been almost romantic, like they were the only people on earth, not bound by social convention, drawn together only by desire.

Someone's obviously been thinking about this *a lot*.

The next morning, she'd given him her Tiffany ID bracelet with the letters KAT engraved on it. Owen had assumed that was her name, and had fantasized about her all summer. Then, after his first day at St Jude's, he'd actually run into her – *with Rhys*. It turned out his Kat was actually Kelsey Addison Talmadge, Rhys's *girlfriend*. Right after she saw Owen, Kat – or Kelsey, it was still confusing – had broken up with Rhys. She'd shown up at Owen's apartment door, looking more luminescent and beautiful than ever when she told him they could be together now. They had kissed, and had almost gotten together, until Owen realized he couldn't be an asshole to his swim buddy. So he broke up with *her*, telling her it had just been a one-night stand and that he didn't have feelings for her. Now Kat never wanted to speak to him again, and all Owen could do was think about her.

Don't worry, no one really understands what's going on.

'Great! Well, gentlemen, you'll get your RSVPs in the mail soon, so look out for 'em. And get ready to get actioned!'

Doesn't he mean *auctioned*?

Coach blew his whistle, signaling the swimmers' dismissal. One by one the guys trailed out of the office and back into the locker room, some pausing to appraise their furry beards and mustaches in the steamed-up mirrors. Rhys plopped down on a creaky wooden bench. He needed a moment. All he could think about was the swim team benefit last year, at the Plaza ballroom, where Kelsey had worn a beautiful green organza gown and he'd twirled her on the dance floor, and they'd been so happy, and, *oh* . . . A small tear formed and dripped out of the corner of his eye, splashing on the damp tiles of the floor.

'Are you *crying*?' Hugh asked as he walked by, his swim bag slung over his shoulder. Hugh was perpetually single and had already settled into a jaded bachelor routine, complete with a maroon smoking jacket he wore at the parties he hosted at his parents' Park Avenue penthouse.

'It's just chlorine,' Rhys lied, roughly swiping at his

brown eyes with the back of his hand. It was one thing to be a hairy loser, but to be a hairy, *crying* loser?

This season on NBC: *The Biggest Hairy Crying Loser.*

'No, it's not chlorine.' Hugh stood back and assessed the situation, then plopped down next to Rhys. 'You're obsessing over Kelsey,' he said, as if he had just completed a very complicated mathematical proof.

Rhys was silent. It was obvious – why fucking try to pretend?

'Dude, you're miserable. You've been low for weeks. You haven't even been swimming well. No offense.' Hugh put a tender hand on Rhys's shoulder, as if this pep talk was really helping. 'You have to win her back.' Hugh nodded sagely.

'Yeah!' Ken Williams cried in between bites of a Snickers power bar. His misshapen teeth were caked in chocolate, and flecks of the candy rained down on Rhys's sweatshirt.

Rhys looked from Hugh to Ken miserably. Win Kelsey back? Yeah, right. Maybe he should just give up, eat a million calories a day, and become some fat, hairy ex-swimmer. He could move from the city, live in a cabin in the woods, and raise yaks. He'd have his favorite osetra caviar and sea salt caramels delivered daily from Dean & DeLuca, and he'd never have to think about girls again.

Tempting.

'Thanks, guys.' Rhys stood up and got ready to leave, not bothering to wait for Owen. Watching girls fall all over him was just *another* reminder of Rhys's pathetic singledom.

'Wait!' Ken pulled Rhys's sweatshirt back urgently and Rhys stopped, trying to rein in his rising sense of annoyance. 'I'm telling you, when my girlfriend Stephanie broke up with me, it turned out she was just playing hard to get.'

Rhys rolled his eyes. Ken Williams's only girlfriend to date had been a girl he met at a fat camp in Massachusetts last summer. If Rhys had to hear one more time how Ken had gotten her back by raiding the dining hall and stealing the whole camp's stash of fat-free brownies for her, he was going to hurl.

'I know,' Rhys said shortly. The guys' support was sweet and everything, but he *really* didn't think they could help him.

'No, really, dude, you have to try to win her back, or else you *know* Jenkins is just going to try to hump you,' Hugh snorted. Chadwick, hearing his name, scurried away from the group to safety, still in his Speedo. 'I mean, you're hot, you're smart, you're this whole big package.' Rhys blushed and turned away again. 'Not *that* package.' Hugh laughed. 'Anyway, maybe she's feeling inferior.'

'What?' Rhys was skeptical. Somehow he couldn't imagine Kelsey, a brilliant painter whose work had already been featured in professional Manhattan galleries, feeling inferior about anything.

'Yeah.' Hugh nodded knowingly. 'It's like some sort of projection. Chicks do all this crazy psychological shit.'

Someone's been watching too much *Dr. Phil.*

Rhys looked at the rest of the guys, who had all drifted toward the conversation. They were nodding. Then Chadwick started chanting, in his alto voice that sounded like a choirboy's at St Patrick's Cathedral, *Rhys, Rhys, Rhys.* One by one the boys joined in, and Coach emerged from his office, nodding in silent approval. Rhys stood up on the wobbly bench and nodded to all of them. They all believed in him. *He* just had to believe in himself.

'I'll get her back!' he announced grandly. He noticed an eighty-something-year-old guy in a saggy Speedo, early for the Y's open swim session, and winced. He couldn't let his *youth* just pass him by!

'Awesome – shaving party tomorrow!' Hugh crowed. Rhys glared at him. Couldn't the guys just let the hair-growing-until-Rhys-got-action project go? Hugh shrugged. 'You need to get her back and *do* something, man.'

One by one, the guys filed out, high-fiving Rhys. They seemed to stand taller, knowing their leader was back in the game.

'Hey.' Rhys approached the next row of lockers, where Owen was wordlessly rolling his swim towel into a tight snake.

'Hey,' Owen responded woodenly. Of course the whole reason he'd told Kat – Kelsey – they couldn't be together was so she'd go back to Rhys and all would be right with the world. But then when a week had passed and nothing had happened, he'd felt . . . well, *relieved*. The idea of Rhys trying to win her back made Owen hurt in an area suspiciously close to his heart.

'I didn't see you over there. Do you think I should do it?'

Owen took in his friend's furrowed brow. Rhys needed Kelsey. That much was clear. Finally, Owen nodded.

'Yeah, man. Win her back.' He folded his towel into a smaller and smaller ball.

'So, are you excited about the auction? You've certainly got enough girls who'll bid for you,' Rhys ventured.

'Nah.' Owen shrugged and zipped his bag. 'I'm taking a break to focus on swimming. Girls slow me down.'

Rhys nodded. Something seemed *off* about his friend, but he couldn't figure out what. On the surface, Owen looked great, and his times were amazing. But he hadn't seemed like *himself*.

'Okay, see you . . .' Rhys said uncertainly to Owen's retreating back. Was there something he didn't know?

And does he really want to know it?

she's already a triplet, but *b* may have found a twin . . .

'What can I do for you, baby?' a kindly white-haired bartender asked as soon as Baby opened the door to a nondescript bar on the Upper West Side on Tuesday after school. It was the same story everywhere. Partly because she was so tiny, people often called her 'baby,' which made it sort of awkward when they eventually found out that was her real name. It usually bugged her, but this bartender looked like a skinny, European version of Santa Claus, and had probably worked at the bar for at least thirty years. Possibly wearing the same shirt, Baby realized. Stains dotted the white fabric like constellations at the planetarium.

'Um, a Jack and Coke.' Baby nodded definitively. She played with one of the bar napkins, idly folding it into smaller and smaller pieces.

'Hey!' Sydney Miller clomped up to the bar behind Baby and sat down. She was wearing knee-high lace-up Doc Martens with enormous platform soles that made her stand almost six feet tall, a black lace skirt, and a black wifebeater that read, I SLAP MY OWN ASS. With her lanky frame, dark bobbed hair, and rectangular-shaped glasses, Sydney looked like she belonged in a coffee shop in Williamsburg drinking some sort of organic, fair trade coffee, not at an old-school Irish pub on the Upper West Side. Baby grinned in relief. When Mrs McLean had sentenced her to work on *Rancor*, she had assumed she'd have to meet with some poetry-loving, prairie-skirt-wearing girl who'd want to debate the merits of sestinas versus pantoums. But she'd immediately recognized Sydney as the one girl at Constance she could actually imagine being friends with.

'You're Baby, right?' Sydney plopped onto the stool next to her without waiting for an answer. 'Can I have a Guinness? It's freaking hot outside!' she called to the bartender, wiping away the beads of sweat on her fair forehead. 'You know, I didn't realize that you and Avery were sisters. You seem so different,' Sydney exclaimed, peering curiously at Baby. She grabbed Baby's drink and took a liberal swig.

'Jack and Coke,' she observed, clearly impressed. 'So, what are you doing with that J.P. Ridiculous Cash dude? Are you together?'

Baby smiled at the randomness of Sydney's all-over-the-place monologue. 'I guess so. I mean, yes,' she said firmly. She took a sip of her drink, enjoying the way the sweetness of the soda mixed with the burning sensation of the whiskey. She thought about how J.P.'s lips tasted like eucalyptus and Marvis toothpaste. She took another sip of her drink. She could like whiskey *and* eucalyptus.

Just as long as she doesn't mix them together.

'Interesting. So what's it like dating the mini mogul?'

Sydney popped some of the stale-looking orange-cracker-and-peanut mix on the bar into her mouth. It looked at least as old as the bartender. 'Yum,' Sydney commented, her tongue ring flashing in the dim light of the bar. Besides the bartender, they were the only ones there. It sort of felt like a secret clubhouse.

'He's great,' Baby said simply. She felt surprisingly shy talking about J.P., even though she wasn't shy about her feelings for him. Ever since they'd kissed yesterday, they'd quickly assumed the roles of boyfriend and girlfriend. She had woken up this morning to J.P. calling her. He'd e-mailed her a sweet note during study hall, and had even made dinner reservations for tonight, before Baby told him about this meeting. It was super romantic, but a huge change from her last boyfriend, Tom, whose idea of a romantic gesture was not letting Baby's phone calls go straight to voice mail. It was going to take a little while to get used to this whole perfect-boyfriend thing. But Baby certainly *could* get used to it.

Couldn't we all.

'Well, good for him, I guess. I don't know him at all, but I know he was dating Jack Laurent. Could you imagine dating that bitch?' Sydney shuddered, as if she were really considering a relationship with Jack.

Sweet. They could wear matching message tees: I'M A BITCH and SHE'S MY BITCH.

'Why *is* everyone at Constance so bitchy?' Baby asked, genuinely curious. She knew they were supposed to talk about *Rancor*, but it was nice to talk to another girl who seemed to have the same attitude that she did.

'I think it's because all-female communities are inher-ently unstable, especially in the presence of heteronormative cultural forces.' Sydney chewed thoughtfully and shrugged as she wiped orange crumbs off her ruby red lipstick. 'That's why I wanted to meet here. Once school is over, I just like to be as far away from Constance as possible.'

'I know what you mean. I'm still sort of on probation,' Baby admitted. 'Actually, Mrs McLean suggested I work on *Rancor*. Which I'm totally excited about,' she said quickly, not wanting to offend Sydney. 'I'm just relieved I didn't get kicked out. I don't know what I'd do.' Baby shrugged and thought about it. What would she have done? Become a professional dog walker? Bitchy culture or not, Constance Billard was one of the best schools in Manhattan, and definitely Baby's best option.

'Are you kidding? They wouldn't kick anyone out. They're so scared about the endowment,' Sydney snorted. 'And no problem about *Rancor*. I got roped in for the same reason.'

'You did?' Baby asked, realizing she was now on her second drink. How'd that happen?

Heteronormative cultural forces, perhaps?

'Yeah, I sort of had an incident with my English class last year. I did this campaign where I put these RESIST THE PATRIARCHY stickers in everyone's blue books before exams, since all we read all year are dumb old white-man novels. I just wanted to raise the issue. It was totally a good idea.' She sighed tragically. 'So, I'm glad you're helping me. And *help* is the operative word. You *have* to look at this shit.' Sydney smiled ruefully as she rooted through her orange Brooklyn Industries messenger bag. Baby realized she had the same one in lime green at home.

Great minds think . . . alike?

'So, anyway, I brought a bunch of submissions,' Sydney

began dubiously, sorting through handwritten sheets of paper interspersed with printouts. 'This one's my favorite. It's deep, though. Don't cry or anything,' she warned, passing Baby a creased piece of notebook paper.

Baby smoothed the piece of paper onto the dark oak of the bar. The place was beginning to fill up, and a few dorky-looking guys had plunked down next to them. They had ordered a pitcher of beer and were spiritedly discussing Aristotle like they actually cared. She liked this bar, even though it smelled like a combination of Lysol and beer. The only other bars she'd been to in New York City were ones Avery had chosen, which were always super crowded and super loud and specialized in absurdly colorful drinks that tasted like Froot Loops.

Baby began to read the bubbly pink-pen handwriting on the page.

STAIRWAY TO BARNEYS
Barneys is my favorite store;
Whenever I go I always want more.
From makeup to lingerie, Marc Jacobs to Sevens,
It's like each floor is a stairway to heaven.
But it's more than what my platinum AmEx can buy.
The store is like a metaphor: it teaches me how to try.
From a Balenciaga tote to Phillip Lim's smaller size
Barneys has taught me to keep my eyes on the prize.

Baby snorted and started to cough. The guy next to her whacked her on the back with his dog-eared copy of Plato's *Republic*.

'Thanks,' she sputtered.

Sydney smiled gleefully. 'Can we get two shots of

bourbon?' she yelled down to the bartender. 'My treat. You need a drink after reading that.'

'You made that up. You had to have written that.' Baby giggled in disbelief as she balled up a napkin and threw it at Sydney, already feeling kind of drunk. Sure, she doubted the intellect of some of her Constance classmates, but no one could ever write something that sucked *so* bad, right? It had to be a joke, or a satire?

Sydney threw the napkin back at her. 'Nope. Came in through the submissions box today. It's this sophomore, Florida Harris. Her dad is that weatherman with the toupee on *The Early Show*?'

Baby groaned. Back in Nantucket, she, Avery, and Owen would always watch that station just to see the epic, glacier-like journey his toupee would make from the top of his head to halfway down his forehead.

Sydney cracked an evil grin. 'Need another shot?'

'Maybe.' Baby giggled. Just then, her slim red Nokia buzzed. She opened it.

MISSING YOU, BEAUTIFUL, X J.P., read the letters on the tiny screen.

'Boyfriend?'

'Yeah.' Baby nodded, not sure what to write back. MISS YOU TOO, HANDSOME? Ew.

'That's cool. My boyfriend's actually coming to meet us here any minute. I hope that's okay,' Sydney said, clearly not worried about whether it was okay or not. 'So, anyway, this is the material we have to work with, so *any* ideas on how to make it remotely readable would be amazing.' Sydney laughed, finishing off Baby's drink. She put the poems back in her messenger bag and set it down on the bar's sticky floor. Clearly, the meeting was over.

Just then, a tall, super-skinny boy with wiry, Brillo pad–like brown hair held back with an '80s-style sweatband walked over to Sydney and Baby.

'Hey lover.' He leaned in and kissed Sydney. Baby politely looked away.

'Webber,' the guy said, holding out his hand. Baby fought the urge not to laugh. *Webber?* It sounded like a name a toddler would give his stuffed duck.

'I know, his name sucks.' Sydney rolled her eyes at Webber. 'Webber, this is Baby, which is her real name, so please don't make fun of it. She's helping me out with the loser lit mag. Webber goes to Columbia,' Sydney explained.

'Nice to meet you,' Webber said, squeezing onto the same stool as Sydney. 'So does that mean you guys are finally going to cover UR?'

'Uhrrrr?' Baby asked stupidly. She wondered if it was some new pronoun or something.

'Underground Response,' Sydney explained. 'It's this cool group Webber founded with some other Columbia people, but now it's bigger. They try to make a statement by doing improv or performance art in public places,' she rattled off. 'That's sort of what I was trying to start with my sticker campaign last year. But, you know, it's hard to do these things without support.'

Baby nodded politely. That actually sounded sort of cool, and way more fun than the stuffy society benefit circuit Avery couldn't wait to be a part of.

'We're doing a naked run tonight through Grand Central. We go, and then when the train times are announced, we take off our pants and run to the platform. It's all about how we deal with living in an overly hurried society. Do you want to come?' Webber asked Baby. 'Syd's coming.'

'Not tonight . . .' Baby said slowly, an idea forming in her head. She glanced at Sydney.

'Oh my God, let's do some sort of artsy, *Paper*-style photomontage with UR for *Rancor*! I can't believe I didn't think about that before!' Sydney exclaimed, whipping out a notebook and writing furiously. 'I could photograph it. Can you write something to go with it?' Even though it was a question, Sydney barked it like an order.

Baby nodded. Why not?

'Constance is ready for that?' Webber clutched his chest in mock horror.

'It's even better if they're not ready.' Sydney grinned wickedly.

'I'd love to do whatever – writing or photographing, it doesn't matter to me,' Baby offered, surprising herself. Except for ridiculous camera phone pictures she used to take with her boyfriend Tom back in Nantucket, she'd never really been into photography. But now that she'd decided to stay in New York, it was as if she was seeing everything in a new light.

And with naked performance art in her future, people will be looking at *her* differently, too!

confessions aren't limited to the dance floor

After school on Tuesday, Jack tromped up the rickety stairs to the garret, a collection of rooms atop the spacious town house she and her mother used to occupy. The garret had been built in the 1800s to house servants, but Jack and her mother, Vivienne, had always used it as a storage space for last season's castoffs. Now, the rooms served as a makeshift apartment, furnished with a mishmash of Vivienne's biggest decorating mistakes.

Jack flung down her purse on the spinach-colored couch from the mid-'80s and exhaled loudly. She heard the sounds of Edith Piaf emanating through the paper-thin walls of the apartment and her mother's out-of-tune voice warbling 'Je Ne Regrette Rien.' Fan-fucking-tastic. Maman was home.

'Chérie!' Vivienne wobbled into the living room as if on cue. She had been a celebrated prima ballerina in her twenties, until an affair with Charles Laurent, the ambassador to France, had turned into an unexpected pregnancy, a hasty marriage, and a move to New York City. After her even hastier divorce, Vivienne had channeled her energies into shopping at Chanel, hosting benefit tea parties for the School of American Ballet, and critiquing Jack's ballet performances. Since Charles had cut them off, citing Vivienne's irresponsibility with money, she had seemed to age almost overnight. Her wild red hair stuck out all over and her neck was wrapped in several Hermès scarves of different colors. She looked like Little Edie from *Grey Gardens*, the horrific documentary Jack had watched about Jackie O's crazy cousins who lived in an Easthampton mansion with six million cats.

At least the garret doesn't have *room* for six million cats.

'What do you think about television?' Vivienne practically pushed Jack down on a moth-eaten red velvet chair and cocked her head expectantly.

'It'd be nice to *have* one,' Jack returned spitefully. In actuality, she'd never watched much television. She had never understood the point of watching other people's lives. It seemed like something for people whose lives weren't naturally fabulous.

'No, darling, I'm not asking about your thoughts on a *television* in our house. We're artists: We don't watch art – we *are* art,' Vivienne said dramatically. She clapped her hands together, as if she were about to put on a show.

The Dance of the Seven Veils?

'They want me. Paris wants me. For a television show. It's my moment. *C'est mon retour!*' Vivienne's eyes shone as she eyed herself in the ugly gilt-frame mirror she'd bought at a Sotheby's auction a million years ago. She didn't even notice Jack giving her the evil eye. Great. So her mom would run back to Paris and be on some totally embarrassing trashy French drama while Jack would have to learn *responsibility* in a musty attic that looked like the freaking Housing Works thrift shop on Seventy-seventh Street.

'Which means I must get ready for Paris. There is much to be done. Oh, Jacqueline.' Vivienne grinned, rising to her full height of five foot zero. 'Ve vill get rid of ze carbs, and I am going to put myself on a regimen. And it'll be good for you, *ma chérie*. Carbs make you soft.' Vivienne flung her hands open as if she were performing for an invisible audience. Jack stood up. She had had enough of all of these 'you need to learn how to suffer' speeches.

'I have homework,' Jack mumbled, stomping into her bedroom. She went over to the one tiny window above her twin bed and looked down into what used to be their garden. The trees were still a lush green, but in a few weeks the leaves would all start to fall off, making the view totally depressing. Maybe in a few weeks, she wouldn't even *be* in New York City anymore. She stood up, performed a few deep pliés, then extended her leg upward. Was it her imagination, or was she not as flexible as she used to be?

Jack pulled out her Treo and called Genevieve. They used to be best friends, and even though sometimes Genevieve's pseudo-involvement with the Hollywood scene totally annoyed her, at least she was *someone*.

'Can I come over?' Jack asked when Genevieve answered. She felt a tiny bit lame having to ask. This was reason #3487 why it sucked not to have a boyfriend. With J.P., she'd never had to *ask* to come over – she'd just gone.

'Whatever.' Genevieve sighed lazily into the phone. That was pretty much as enthusiastic as Genevieve got. Jack walked out of her bedroom and slammed the door, but her mother was too busy posing in front of the mirror to notice.

Twenty minutes and one harrowing subway ride later, Genevieve opened the door to the modest but meticulously maintained all-white apartment on Third Avenue she lived in with her mom, a former model who now mainly appeared in *Lifetime* television movies. Genevieve was still wearing her Constance skirt, rolled up so high it practically showed her Cosabella-covered ass, and a see-through light pink camisole. She looked like an alcoholic divorcée, minus the wrinkles. Wordlessly, Genevieve passed Jack an oversize Riedel glass filled to the brim with red wine.

'Thanks,' Jack said gratefully, swilling the liquid before daintily setting the glass on the counter. She looked around the small apartment, which was covered in photographs of Genevieve's mom. She cringed when her eyes landed on the large front-and-center semi-nude photo of Genevieve's mom when she'd been pregnant with Genevieve, which hung above the arched brick fireplace. Ew. Her own mom might be crazy, but at least she wasn't *tacky*.

'So, what's going on?' Genevieve demanded. She seemed a little buzzed, and her lips were tinted red from the wine. Genevieve had overly highlighted blond hair, a tiny pert nose (courtesy of three deviated septum surgeries, one for every summer she'd spent in LA with her film director dad), boobs that had gotten bigger every single summer her nose got smaller, and long brown eyelashes that sort of made her look like a camel. When she was eight, she'd starred in a Disney movie, but then had 'outgrown her cute phase.' Now, she occasionally still acted in soap operas or guest starred on *Law & Order* episodes, but she was still not so secretly waiting for her big break.

'I hate J.P. and the slutty boho girl.' Jack sighed and

leaned into the all-white couch, trying to avoid looking at the picture of Genevieve's naked, pregnant mom.

'Whatever. Honestly, I know it sucks to break up with someone.' Genevieve sat down next to her and sighed heavily.

No, you don't, Jack thought. Genevieve's longest relationship ever – with one of her dad's dumb B-list teen actor connections – had lasted all of two weeks.

'But, honestly, is it really just J.P.? What's going on with you recently? You used to be this *force.* Now you don't want to go out with us, you don't come to Barneys, you kiss Avery Carlyle's ass even though you said you hated her . . . Are you, like, having some type of secret affair with her doorman or something?' Genevieve's eyes lit up at the thought of an illicit affair. Obviously, the convoluted soap opera plotlines she'd been involved in had affected her sense of reality.

'I'm not kissing Avery's ass.' Jack laughed awkwardly and choked down the wine. She thought about last Wednesday, when the strap of Avery's purse had broken and Jack had actually *carried her books* for her. She'd tried to reserve her sucking-up time for when she was alone with Avery, but apparently her friends had noticed. What if they decided she was a total loser and officially excluded her from the group? She had to do *something.*

'Who do you think called the cops at her party?' Jack smirked, pleased when a shocked look spread over Genevieve's face.

'*You* did? But then why are you being so buddy-buddy with her? Is it, like, to get to her hot brother or something?' Genevieve called behind her as she stalked to the kitchen for a refill.

'Actually, it's . . .' Jack trailed off as she cast about for a good lie, her lower lip trembling. She'd wanted nothing more than to talk to someone – anyone – about her problems for so long. 'My dad cut me and my mom off. He sold our house, we're living upstairs in the fucking *attic*, and Avery found out. I didn't want anyone to know,' Jack said in a rush of words while Genevieve was still in the kitchen. It was easier to say it when she was in the next room.

'Seriously?' Genevieve stopped in her tracks, holding one bottle of wine in each hand.

'Yeah.' Jack shrugged her shoulders defensively. She *really* hadn't thought this conversation through. Now Genevieve was going to tell everyone, and they'd host some type of *benefit* for her or something.

'Whatever.' Genevieve sat back down on the couch. 'My dad does that all the time. Especially if one of his movies tanks.' She expertly plunged a corkscrew into the center of the bottle of vintage 1980 L'Evangile bordeaux, unscrewed it, and splashed the liquid liberally into Jack's still-full glass. 'Why do you think my mom has played Tori Spelling's mom in, like, ten television movies? God, men can be such *assholes*, you know?' She shrugged sympathetic-ally. 'I just don't understand why you had to keep it some big secret from us. What, you think we'd dump you because of your asshole father?' Genevieve leaned in and hugged Jack. Jack gratefully embraced her back. Genevieve's boobs really were huge. Hugging her was like hugging Dr McFadden, her freshman year geometry teacher, whose gravity-defying chest had always been a subject of speculation. Jack let out a small sob. It just felt so good to be taken care of for once.

'Oh my God.' Genevieve rolled her eyes in exasperation as she drew back. 'Don't get all melodramatic on me.' She hiccupped and slammed the entire wine bottle on the table. Jack smiled in giddy relief, trying to stop a huge grin from forming. She didn't want it to be obvious how pathetic she was.

'Let's go out and *really* have drinks. There's tons of cheap bars around here. Sometimes slumming it is the way to go.' Genevieve pulled off her sweater and examined her pink Cosabella cami–clad self in the mirror. 'Totally trashy.' She nodded happily at her reflection.

Jack considered. It might be fun to just *go out*, even if out was just some lame, sticky-floored frat bar.

'Sure,' she agreed.

As soon as they went outside, a bevy of construction workers on the corner whistled at them.

'Assholes.' Genevieve stuck out her tongue and held up her middle finger but looked a little pleased. Jack nodded wordlessly, even though their hoots and hollers were music to her ears. She felt her old confidence returning. Her family might suck, her housing situation might be a disaster, but this was New York, and she *belonged* here. The city had everything she needed, including flirty bartenders and free drinks.

tea and sympathy

Avery Carlyle walked into the Pierre Hotel on Tuesday afternoon, her navy blue Miu Miu kitten heels clacking across the marble floor. Her meeting with the Constance board of overseers would take place in the rotunda at four o'clock. Avery's noisy footsteps seemed to drown out the piano player in the corner, and she tried to walk discreetly on her tiptoes – the last thing she wanted was to announce her presence to the board by sounding like a freaking Rockette.

As Avery entered the rotunda, she nervously pushed a flyaway strand of blond hair under her favorite thick bejeweled Marc Jacobs headband. Looking around, she realized she was the youngest attendee by *at least* fifty years. The air was thick with the scent of Chanel No. 5, and Avery weaved through the straight-backed gilt chairs, hoping she'd be able to recognize Muffy St Clair. It was hard to tell anyone apart, since all the ladies were clad in black St John power suits, pearls, three-inch heels, and tastefully dyed gray-blond hair practically lacquered three inches above their Botoxed foreheads.

'Avery!' Muffy croaked from a center table. Avery sighed in relief and made her way over, aware that heads were turning to watch her. Muffy slowly shuffled toward Avery with the aid of an elegant cane, and Avery leaned in to gently kiss her on the cheek. 'You're the spitting image of your grandmother. Of course, back then we were dancing on tables, not meeting for tea.' Muffy clicked her tongue ruefully and pressed her dry, apricot-colored lips together as she wrapped her bony fingers around Avery's forearm. 'Come, I can't wait for you to add some young blood to our Constance group.'

'Thank you!' Avery squeaked. 'I mean, that sounds lovely,' she corrected, trying to lower the pitch of her voice so she didn't sound like an over-caffeinated cheerleader.

'What?' Muffy boomed. She leaned in so close to Avery that droplets of spit landed on Avery's ear. 'Whenever I'm at these meetings, I take my hearing aids out. I'd want to murder one of these old biddies if I didn't!' Muffy laughed raucously.

Avery nodded politely and shuffled behind Muffy across the plush cotton candy–colored carpet. For the millionth time, she imagined Grandmother Avery, wherever she was, smiling down on her. *This* was the New York City she had always imagined.

Surrounded by septuagenarians?

'Hello!' one of the ladies croaked, holding out a wrinkly hand. 'So, this is what Constance looks like now.' She paused, surveying Avery up and down.

'Excuse me?' Avery asked.

'Don't mind Esther,' Muffy said.

'Here, sit.' Her thick Chanel gold bangles clunked against each other as Avery sat down between Esther and some lady who was practically falling asleep in her plate of scones.

'Thanks,' Avery responded shyly. She neatly smoothed her Constance skirt over her knees and made sure to sit up straight. The waiter came over with a delicate teapot and poured one cup. Avery was suddenly reminded of her disastrous first attempt at popularity, when she'd planned a tea party her first week of school and invited all her Constance classmates, but no one had shown up.

Seems like she targeted the wrong audience.

'Well, we have a lot of work to do,' Muffy addressed the group, clapping her hands together. Avery noticed her discreetly pop something into her left ear as she pretended to smooth a wayward lock of orangish-red hair into place. Her thin, brittle nails were painted a garish red. 'To begin with, who knows *anything* about Camilla Hoover's *dreadful* visit to Dr Brower?'

'Oh, I know.' Esther looked down dolefully as the rest of the ladies followed suit. Avery cast her eyes down too.

'That's terrible,' Avery murmured in what she hoped was an appropriately somber tone of voice. Camilla must have been diagnosed with some life-threatening illness. Avery shifted uncomfortably as she surveyed the elegant scene around her. A harpist played in the background, and the walls were designed to resemble those of a European cathedral. It was beautiful, but very *mature*.

Read: boring.

'Bloody terrible,' Esther seconded, screeching into Avery's ear. 'How much Restylane could they have possibly pumped in her? The woman already looked like a gerbil!'

'It's a step up from her usual look, that's for sure,' a dour-looking woman with curly black hair said as she drummed her pink nails against the table. Her gnarled hands reminded Avery of the ancient tree in their backyard in Nantucket.

'Well, you'd think someone would have directed her to the proper surgeon. And now she's pretending *nothing* has happened.' Muffy shook her head sadly in the universal way girls and women do when they want to sound sympathetic but are really just being bitchy. Avery knew that gesture all too well. She looked up, her eyes darting among Muffy, Esther, and the rest of the innocent-seeming ladies. Were they *gossiping*? Then she noticed the fragile-looking, completely silver-haired woman across from her, stealthily pouring liquid from an engraved flask into her fragile, rose-painted teacup. *And drinking?*

See? We're all the same.

The woman across from her noticed Avery's piercing gaze. She held the flask up, raising her heavily penciled eyebrow in offering. Avery felt her face flush and shook her head.

'Well, I think we should move on to the business at hand,' Esther began. Avery relaxed. Finally, the real meeting was going to start. She couldn't wait to hear more about the board's plans for Constance, and to chime in with her opinions. 'Let's start with attendance.'

'I can do that for you,' one woman said in a raspy smoker's voice. She sounded like she'd inhaled a whole chimney. 'Not here: Ticky Bensimmon-Heart.' Avery played with her gold locket thoughtfully. Ticky Bensimmon-Heart? The name sounded familiar. Avery racked her brain, trying to figure out where she had heard it before. Wasn't she the editor of *Metropolitan* magazine? *Metropolitan* was the coolest New York City–based magazine, combining fashion, Manhattan society gossip, and criticism all in one package. The magazine had never tried to go beyond the city, since Ticky ruled it with an iron fist and reportedly believed that nothing worth covering happened outside Manhattan (with the possible exceptions of Paris and Milan).

'Thinks she's too good for us, then always swoops in and steals all the photo ops at our benefits.' Muffy sighed sadly and took Avery's hand in hers. 'Well, I'd like to introduce someone very special to everyone. Does this little lady look familiar? Because this is none other than Avery Carlyle, granddaughter of our *own* Avery.' Murmurs flew up and down the table. 'Can you be a doll and introduce yourself? Loudly?' Muffy reminded her.

'Hi, I'm Avery Carlyle. I hope I live up to your expectations and those of my grandmother Avery,' she said shyly.

All the women clapped, the drama of Ticky Bensimmon-Heart's nonattendance apparently forgotten.

'So, to begin with, let's discuss the uniform policy at Constance,' Muffy announced. Avery perked up. She *loved* talking about uniforms. It'd be great if they could lose the seersucker warm weather skirts. It was only a few weeks into the school year, and Avery was already sick of them. She sketched out a simple flare skirt with a military-style jacket in her pink Filofax. Maybe the skirt could be pin-striped? Or some adorable plaid?

'Last month we agreed the color of the skirt should change. Today we need to decide: navy blue or midnight blue?'

Avery frowned. It had taken them a whole month to decide whether the skirt color needed to change? And what was the difference between navy and midnight, anyway?

'I say midnight blue. Objections?' Muffy asked the group, as if she clearly didn't expect there to be any. The woman next to Avery was now snoring, a small trail of drool trailing down her chin.

'Midnight is awfully sophisticated. These are little girls we're talking about. We don't want them looking . . . *loose*, like those awful French girls at L'École.' A woman with four Cartier necklaces shook her head sadly. Avery tuned out, pulling apart a thick, stale scone. It was heavier than a hand grenade.

As the ladies continued to argue the merits of navy versus midnight, Avery wondered what Jack, Genevieve, and Sarah Jane were doing. Even though she was thrilled to have this position, she kind of wished she could just be sitting on the steps of the Met, talking about life and surveying the St Jude's guys who walked past for boyfriend potential. Avery had never had a *real* boyfriend. Sure, there were plenty of boys she'd had crushes on, and a few she'd kissed. But that was back in Nantucket, and when the relationship seemed to be going to the next level something had always gone wrong. She couldn't wait to meet a sophisticated, totally hot Upper East Sider. Now, with Constance Billard's most popular girls as her best friends, it was destined to happen. The only question was, *when*?

'Avery, what do you think?' Muffy clamped her hand down on Avery's forearm, yanking her out of her reverie.

'Midnight,' Avery chirped guiltily. Was it obvious she'd been zoning out?

'What?' Muffy looked confused. 'Honey, we asked you if you saw Dinah nip from her flask. She does that some-times, so we *do* need to know, or else she falls asleep in the powder room.'

'Oh, I didn't notice.' Avery blushed furiously as she realized the lady who'd been sitting next to her was no longer there.

'Esther, would you mind going to fetch Dinah? She's probably in the usual spot,' Muffy said sadly. 'Next time, Avery, will you watch out for her?'

Avery nodded, feeling slightly annoyed. So now her job was to look after the old alcoholic lady? This wasn't what she had signed up for. Talk about false pretenses. The board of overseers was nothing more than a group of old society ladies who drank, gossiped, and accomplished next to nothing at their meetings. Discreetly, she tried to check her Rolex, hoping she might have time to meet up with the girls before it got dark.

'Okay, darling.' Muffy seemed to read her mind. 'It was a pleasure to have you here. You're a *very* valuable member.' One by one each of the women nodded. 'You can run off if you'd like. I think we need to continue this meeting in the lounge, over a cordial.' Muffy's brown eyes twinkled merrily. 'Of course, you're more than welcome to join us.'

'No thank you!' Avery smiled to the women and stood up quickly. She didn't even *want* to know what they'd talk about once alcohol was involved.

r would do anything for love . . .
but he won't do that

Rhys Sterling paused in the red-carpeted front hallway of his town house, adjusting his slate gray Thomas Pink tie. The ornate front room was decorated with heavy oak and walnut furniture taken from various estates around England. Tonight the Sterlings were having a formal dinner, which his prim and proper mother insisted on three times a week. She had met Rhys's father, Lord Algernon Sterling, during her junior year abroad from Vassar on an Oxford exchange program. As soon as they were married and she'd taken the title of Lady Sterling, she'd reinvented herself as European royalty. With her impeccable manners and penchant for wearing large hats like Queen Elizabeth, everyone politely overlooked the fact that she was actually from Greenwich, Connecticut, and not Greenwich, UK.

Rhys entered the dining room and held out his hand for his father to shake. Algernon wordlessly shook it, then held up a small glass of sherry in a vague toast. Rhys sat down in his seat, feeling lonely. Kelsey always used to come to formal dinners, and something about her infectious enthusiasm made them almost *fun*. Even Lord Sterling, the tall, silver-haired, bespectacled CEO of a major publishing empire, always said he had a cracking good time with her. He even put his BlackBerry away when Kelsey was talking, a rare feat indeed.

'Darling, you made it home!' Lady Sterling cooed from the other end of the table, as if Rhys had just swum across the Atlantic Ocean and not walked from the Ninety-second Street Y. Rhys shrugged and glanced up at his mom. Her all-white hair was pulled back regally into a chignon. Her hair had been that color even before Rhys was born, but her skin was completely wrinkle-free. She looked like a wig-wearing Nicole Kidman.

'I'm so happy the family is here together. But, of course, it would have been delightful if Kelsey were here as well. She's always a great addition to our discussions,' Lady Sterling said, peering at Rhys through her half-moon eyeglasses. Rhys shifted uncomfortably. His mom was always enthusiastic, but today she seemed a little giddy. He was suddenly reminded of the time she'd filmed an episode of *Christmas with Lady Sterling* and accidentally over-proportioned a recipe for a holiday punch, pouring two bottles instead of two cups of gin. Throughout the episode she'd sipped daintily from the punch bowl as she tittered about what a happy holiday it was.

'Yeah, she couldn't make it,' Rhys mumbled as he smoothed a thick white linen napkin on his lap. Anka, their stern Romanian maid, set his plate down with a clatter.

'I have an announcement,' Lady Sterling trilled as Anka skulked off. '*Town & Country* wants to do a shoot with me and your father. Apparently they're doing this great "English Abroad and In Love" spread. Doesn't that sound enchanting?' She fluttered her eyelashes at Lord Sterling, who was sneaking a look at his BlackBerry under the table.

'Quite right, darling.' He nodded quickly.

Lady Sterling beamed. 'Of course, you and Kelsey will be in the shot with us. Even if she isn't from the UK . . . or even the Continent,' Lady Sterling noted darkly. Then she brightened. 'But she's not like those typical American girls with all the tattoos and bad manners, either.'

'That's not a good idea,' Rhys said automatically, pushing his pistachio-encrusted salmon around his plate. He hadn't told his mom about what had happened with Kelsey. Explaining that she'd dumped him for some other guy would make everybody look bad.

'Are you two having troubles?' Lady Sterling perked up, obviously sensing a topic for her television show.

'It's . . . complicated.' Rhys hesitated. Maybe if he won Kelsey back soon enough – he had every intention of doing so; he just hadn't figured out how – his parents would never need to know they'd been broken up.

His father dropped the spoon he'd been using to chase the peas through his wild mushroom butter. 'So you've been chucked?'

Rhys looked down miserably at his plate. Great. Now his parents knew he'd been dumped, and he'd have to suffer their humiliating pity through a long, formal dinner.

'Oh, don't be silly, my boy!' Lord Sterling stated firmly

as he slammed his spoon and knife against the table. 'The back-and-forth, the chase – it's all part of the game. How do you think I got your mother?' He smirked.

A vague claim to royalty might have had *something* to do with it.

'Oh, Algy!' Lady Sterling giggled, her face turning bright red. Rhys looked up sharply, hoping his parents weren't talking about sex.

'I had to show her how romance worked. I had to put a spell on her.' Lord Sterling smiled broadly, obviously pleased with himself, and held up his wineglass for Anka to refill. Rhys shifted uncomfortably. He didn't like thinking of his father as some winsome lothario, wooing his mother with his 'spells.'

'He did. And that's what you'll have to do with Kelsey,' Lady Sterling declared. She swept over to Rhys and patted his head encouragingly, as if he were one of her five corgis.

Hmm, someone really has a Queen Elizabeth fetish.

'What if you brought her onto *Tea with Lady Sterling*? I could do a whole show on young love. We'd talk to you, we'd talk to her, we'd really get to the root of it. I think it'd help a lot of your schoolmates to watch that.' Lady Sterling nodded thoughtfully.

Rhys loosened his tie and glanced at his father for help. He was all for getting Kelsey back, but announcing it on a national television show was a terrible idea. His mom already played a clip of him when he was five, asking Kelsey to be his Valentine, on February 14 every year. He'd look like an even *bigger* loser if he went on the show and admitted they weren't together anymore. 'Um, thanks, but I think I want to do something more low-key,' Rhys mumbled, unable to believe he was getting dating advice from his parents. As if his life weren't already lame enough.

'Hush, darling. It'll be grand,' Lady Sterling said. 'Algy, give me that.' She gestured to her husband's BlackBerry and furiously typed in a number. Rhys looked on in horror. She wasn't calling *Kelsey*, was she?

Who could say no to Lady Sterling?

'Bob, Lady S here. Listen, I had an idea for the show and needed to discuss. My son and his girlfriend are going through some issues – you know, young love, expectations, all that.' Bob was her flamboyant producer and jumped at the opportunity to do anything over-the-top. 'What if we do a piece on courting, then and now? Rhys could court Kelsey, with maybe some sort of 1890 Gilded Age setup, you know?' Rhys watched as Lady Sterling furrowed her brow in consternation, thinking on the fly.

'Dad?' Rhys asked in desperation. His father was watching Lady Sterling in fascination, a smile playing on his lips. Great. So everyone thought his life was a fucking comedy.

All the world is *a stage.*

'Okay, that sounds terrific.' Lady Sterling nodded crisply, handing back the BlackBerry to her husband.

'Rhys, it's all settled.' She smiled. 'So here's what Bob and I are thinking: To intro the segment, we'll have both of you go on a very stylized, Old New York–type outing. I think that's the best way to really bring the issue of contemporary society into play. What do you think, dear?'

'No,' Rhys practically shouted. 'I mean . . . I think I'd

rather do something on my own. Without cameras,' he added sternly.

'Oh.' Lady Sterling looked disappointed. 'But it is *such* a good idea, don't you think? I'll have to find another couple for that. But maybe you and she could just use the space after hours? The views are quite lovely, you know. You could have the band as well. They could play something like, oh, I don't know, "Strangers in the Night." I would have been over the moon if your father had wooed me like that. I just think you need to take time to honestly *reconnect* with each other.' Lady Sterling rubbed her bejeweled hands together as Lord Sterling raised his eyebrows at her.

'Maybe.' Rhys considered. His mother's television studio, overlooking Columbus Circle, had windows on all sides, with amazing views of the city that would look really cool at night. Then again, the entire set was decorated in mauve and taupe, with weird, half-naked angel sculptures all over the walls. It wasn't very *Kelsey*, a girl who'd been born in Williamsburg, Brooklyn, and had only moved to the Upper East Side when her sculptor mom married a wealthy financier. Kelsey was elegant, but she was also very downtown. But Central Park . . . Kelsey liked the park.

In fact, Rhys realized excitedly, the park was really where they'd first fallen in love. Their nannies had been best friends when they were children, and that was always where they'd ended up every day after school. It would be much better to tell Kelsey how he felt with a picnic on the grass than some over-the-top romantic dinner at a stuffy restaurant. That wasn't Kelsey's style. But a casual picnic of her favorite foods, at one of her favorite spots in the park . . .

it just might work. It wouldn't be over-the-top or desperate, but – with luck – it'd show her just how well they fit together and remind her of all the good times they'd spent together over the years.

'May I be excused?' Rhys asked, scraping his chair against the cherry floor before his mother could come up with any *other* ideas. Anka immediately came by to whisk away his practically untouched plate. His brain was working overtime as he tried to come up with the perfect, whimsical, not-trying-too-hard plan. Lady Sterling nodded, quietly humming and rocking in her chair. Lord Sterling was doing the same. It was like they were dancing, separated only by nine feet of the Louis XIV mahogany antique table.

Well, they *do* say the British are reserved.

Rhys tore up the stairs and into his suite of rooms. He ripped off his tie and opened the heavy curtains to let in the remains of the evening sunlight. He picked up a silver frame that Kelsey had given him on their first anniversary. The picture inside was of the two of them kissing, in front of the Romeo and Juliet sculpture next to the Delacorte Theater in the park. They had asked a random tourist walking by to take it, and either because the guy was incompetent or had a vendetta against love, their heads were partially cut off in the picture. Kelsey had laughed when she saw it, and Rhys had instantly loved it too. Even though you couldn't see their eyes, it was the type of artsy picture that Kelsey loved, and showed how *happy* they used to be.

In a weird way, his mom's basic advice was totally on track. They needed to reconnect. Just the two of them. No elaborate plans. After all, they'd been *fine* until Rhys had gone overboard trying to make their first time perfect, complete with roses, candles, and cheesy music. No wonder Kelsey freaked out.

Rhys grinned excitedly. What had he been waiting for? It was time to get her back.

Nothing like a heart-to-heart with your stuffy British parents to get you in the mood.

hey people!

all's fair in love and war

In Dante's *Divine Comedy*, the lustful are punished in the second circle of hell through eternal unrest. Is it just me, or does that sound like a familiar experience for some lonely ladies on the Upper East Side? The trickiest thing about love (or lust – I won't discriminate) is that unlike a vintage Prada clutch, an Aston Martin DB9, or admission to an elite Ivy League institution, real, true, spine-tingling love can't be purchased, sold, or bribed out of anyone. If your boyfriend gets stolen, there's no insurance policy. If you lose your girlfriend, well, there's no magic solution to get her back. Love is a battlefield, after all.

But there are many ways to fight the war. I'm talking to those tragic girls who are searching for love in all the wrong places, trailing a certain slightly hairy guy around like lost little ducklings. Ladies, a tip: have two dozen long-stemmed roses delivered to you during school hours. Look surprised, pleased, and touched all at once when you open the card, then immediately excuse yourself. While everyone will assume that you're scampering off to an afternoon with a mysterious stranger, you can cuddle up under your Frette duvet with a collection of Payard chocolates for a viewing of one of the following: *Dr Zhivago*, *Casablanca*, or *An Affair to Remember*. (Future relationship karma points taken away for viewings of *Titanic*, *Lady and the Tramp*, or any movie starring Hugh Grant.) Two hours later, you'll be feeling properly romanced, and everyone will be buzzing about your secret suitor – meaning it's only a matter of time before one actually materializes.

your e-mail

Q: Dear Gossip Girl:

Or should I say, Gossip Grandma? You are so obviously one of those old ladies in that secret society that, like, owns Constance. You probably hold weird sacrificial rituals with Mrs M and the lunch ladies. I guess they taught you how to use a computer, but why else would you be quoting all these weird lines and making it seem like you're so smart? Why don't you just sign off and hobble to the early bird special at Elaine's or wherever you old people hang out? Haha!

– YoungAndFun

A: Dear YAF,

Interesting theory, but I am as young as they come. Besides, how do *you* know where all the oldies are hanging out?

– GG

Q: 'Sup Big G,

Swim team throw-down's coming up. Who u with? You wanna bid on me?

– Playa

A: Dear Playa,

Thanks for the invitation. I prefer to impulse buy, so I won't make any commitments here and now. But if you've got the goods, I may just be swiping my black AmEx card at the benefit!

– GG

P.S. I assume the 'big G' refers to my personality? I'm actually quite petite.

sightings

R buying an extra-large picnic basket at **Dean & DeLuca** and filling it with truffle-goose foie gras, a Gruyère-and-egg quiche, black-and-white cookies, French-style macaroons, and mocha truffles. Hey, sometimes sugar can cure a broken heart . . . if it doesn't cause a diabetic coma first. **J** and **G** getting ridiculously drunk at dollar beer night at one of those sticky-floored bars that don't card on Second. Sometimes you need a break from the velvet ropes at 1Oak or the Rusty Knot! **B** and her new friend, the pierced, tattooed **S**, streaking through the reading room of the New York City Public Library, trailed by security. Lovely . . . assets, ladies. **A**, with her new besties, **J** and **S.J.**, sipping gimlets on her terrace . . . and **O**, trying to hide out from **S.J.** and **J**. Why so shy? They're just feeling the love. Aren't we all? **H**, **I**, **K**, and some other facial-hair-covered swim team members at **Jackson Hole**, whispering about a teammate over their greasy cheeseburgers. Apparently the word *orientation* was thrown around. Hmm. Is someone new joining the team?

Okay, time for me to head off to David Burke & Donatella, where I'll drink an extra-large hot chocolate by the window and scope out whoever's trying to do a discreet H&M run. Nice try. I'm watching!

You know you love me,

o is welcomed to the team

Owen felt like his heart was about to explode as he ran behind the Met on Thursday afternoon. Kat's apartment was on Fifth Avenue, and even from his position inside the park he could see her sheer lilac curtains fluttering in the mid-September breeze. He sped down Cat's Paw Hill, where Coach had assigned mandatory conditioning drills. Dozens of recreational runners and bikers swarmed around him, following the 6.2-mile loop around the perimeter of the park. As the fifth banana yellow spandex-clad biker whooshed past, Owen sped up. The St Jude's swim team was no joke, and Owen was glad that his every waking moment could be spent in physical activity. He just wished he were doing another *kind* of physical activity.

In your dreams! In mine too.

Just then, he felt a hand clap his back.

'Uh.' He grunted in surprise.

'Dude, lookin' good!' Hugh jeered as he drew alongside Owen.

'Uh, thanks,' Owen replied.

'Oh, I wasn't talking about you,' Hugh apologized, looking rueful. 'I meant the ladies over there.' He nodded at two girls jogging past in tight Seaton Arms tank tops.

'What do you think?' Hugh stroked his beard – not an easy feat while running. The motion always made him look surprisingly thoughtful, as if he were talking about Sartre or Hegel rather than braless girls.

'Go for it,' Owen responded noncommittally. Lately he couldn't get himself to even focus on the girls in front of him. Maybe he *should* become a monk.

'I like your hair thing,' Hugh said companionably. He winked at the Seaton Arms girls as he sped up to pass them.

'Thanks.' Owen readjusted the surprisingly comfortable terry cloth headband he'd swiped from Avery's bathroom to keep the hair off his face. She wore them when she applied her gross-looking mud masks. He shivered, the September wind suddenly cold on his sweaty, shirtless chest.

'So, anyway, I was talking about it with the guys, and it's all right, dude. Just talk to us. Like, look at him – nice, right?' Hugh gestured with his elbow to an orangey-tan guy jogging in what looked like a purple wrestler's uniform.

'What?' Owen asked, confused. Owen knew Hugh liberally mixed vodka with his Gatorade for some Friday post-practice pre-partying, but maybe he'd gotten his bottles mixed up. Or did Hugh know something about him and Kelsey? Owen sped up, noticing Chadwick struggling up the hill, wearing just a Speedo, with the words YOU WANT A PIECE OF ME written on his back in magic marker. He looked like he was about to have a heart attack.

'Lookin' good!' Owen cheered halfheartedly to the unlucky frosh.

'I know who wants a piece of that,' Hugh scoffed, easily catching up with Owen. Together, they sprinted the last quarter-mile over to the Seventy-second Street transverse to meet up with Coach. Despite his borderline alcoholic tendencies, Hugh was actually in pretty good shape.

Coach was standing on the steps leading down to Bethesda Fountain, hitting on a woman who was stretching in tight spandex shorts and a purple tank top.

'So, do you think Coach is hot?' Hugh asked as the two guys walked down the steps together.

'I guess so.' Owen shrugged. He'd never really thought about it.

'So, is that your type?' Hugh asked, giving coach two thumbs up. Coach winked as he placed his hand on the woman's lower back, very close to her ass.

Helping her stretch, obviously.

'Huh?' Owen looked at Hugh. Had he been out in the sun too long?

'We're on the same team, pal.' Hugh nodded knowingly. 'Well, not *that* team, but I'm there for you. We can hug if you want,' he offered. Owen stared at him, confused.

'Dude, I have no idea what the fuck you're talking about,' Owen said finally as they made their way down the steps. Around them, guys from the team had also finished their runs and were milling around, hoping the girls sunning themselves in Malia Mills bikinis might notice them. Technically, it was a little too cold to go shirtless, and the bikini-clad girls all had visible goose bumps on their fadingly tanned stomachs.

'This calls for reinforcements. Hey guys!' Hugh yelled. Several girls walking by looked over curiously as the guys swarmed around Owen. 'Okay, I guess this is an intervention,' Hugh continued, clearly enjoying his moment in the spotlight. 'We talked about it, and it's okay that you're gay.'

'It's . . . what? I'm not gay!' Owen sputtered loudly, causing even more people to turn and stare. He looked at his team members, in case this was some type of weird hazing joke, but no one seemed to be laughing. Instead, they were looking at him with wide-eyed expressions, as if they'd never seen him before. Two guys walking down the steps to the fountain and giving each other bites of their ice cream cones looked over their shoulders and winked.

'I'm not gay,' Owen repeated in exasperation, loudly enough for their benefit. Even Coach had abandoned the stretching woman for this conversation. Owen felt like a caged animal at the zoo. His ears turned bright red. Rhys refused to look him in the eye.

'Dude, are you kidding yourself?' Ken Williams lumbered up and threw a large, sweaty arm around Owen's shoulders. He looked like a lumberjack, or Paul Bunyan. All that was missing were the overalls and a blue ox. 'My sister was watching you at your sister's party a few weeks ago. You totally ignored her and all the other girls. You're never with a girl. Ever,' he added

'. . . style.' Coach blew his whistle, causing . . . to turn and stare. 'I love diversity!' he said . . . looked into the crowd, probably trying to gauge whether that sensitive statement had stirred any interest among the vintage-dress-and-Converse-wearing girls sitting on a nearby step.

'But . . . I'm not . . .' Owen floundered. He didn't have a problem with gay people, but he, personally, was so far from gay, it wasn't even funny. Back in Nantucket, he'd never gone a week without kissing a girl. He had a reputation for it. But here, everything was different. He wasn't his player self, and no one had seen him so much as talking to Kelsey, or any other girl. Looking around the group, it seemed useless even to *try* to correct them. What could he even say? That he wasn't gay, he just had a crush on a top secret girl? Owen sighed in frustration. It was useless. The team had broken from its tight circle and were now chatting in groups of twos and threes.

'I think it's so cool. And, like, dude, swimming? You're gonna get so much ass from the teams we swim against. And if you don't, at least you'll get to look, right? That's, like, if I got to be, like, a locker room attendant at Seaton Arms or something, right?' Hugh's eyes gleamed just imagining it. Owen shook his head numbly. His life was already complicated enough. He didn't need this.

'Hey, it's cool! We'll have to find you a nice guy.' Rhys nodded to him and smiled tightly. So Owen was gay. It was cool. They'd just . . . look for a dude together.

Owen swallowed hard and looked at the crowd. They all seemed genuinely happy about his gayness. Maybe it wasn't so bad. At least now he wouldn't have to worry about people finding out about him and Kelsey. In a way, it was the perfect cover.

Just then a guy in super-tight blue spandex who'd been

hovering nearby passed Owen a piece of paper. It had a hastily scribbled name and phone number on it. The guy winked, then jogged off.

Um, maybe not that great of a cover.

three's company

Avery tumbled exhaustedly into the Carlyles' seventeenth-floor penthouse on Thursday after school. She had just come from another absurd overseers' meeting, this time at Goodman's Café in Bergdorf's, where they'd continued the navy blue versus midnight blue skirt discussion. No *wonder* the uniforms hadn't changed since Avery's mom was at Constance. In between the back-and-forth debate about how midnight blue skirts just weren't *appropriate*, Avery had heard more than she ever needed to know about different types of plastic surgery options (which Muffy called 'refreshers'). Her face had been poked and prodded by the old ladies as they determined, like palm readers, where exactly she could look forward to getting wrinkles. Avery still had a trace of the old-lady smell of baby powder, Creed's Fleurissimo, and stale hard candies on her.

'Anyone home?' Avery called, her voice echoing in the living room, which was still bare except for some ultra-modern Jonathan Adler club chairs and a low-slung couch. She wrinkled her nose. She had hoped they'd be living in Grandmother Avery's town house on Sixty-first between Madison and Park, but the lawyers who were appraising the estate had practically freaking moved in. Now that they were in this apartment for the foreseeable future, it could at least be properly decorated. She heard the sound of Edie's Buddhist chanting music coming from her studio. 'Hello?' she called again. She just wanted to talk to someone, preferably someone *normal*.

And wrinkle-free?

'Outside!' she heard Baby yell. Avery shrugged off her boring black Loro Piana cashmere cardigan and threw it carelessly on the couch. Their cat, Rothko, meowed in indignation and jumped off the couch, rubbing his black and white fur against Avery's bare leg.

'Hey kitty,' she murmured. She paused for a second and buried her face in Rothko's soft fur. She'd never been so tired in her life. She stalked into the cavernous kitchen and flung open the cabinets. Her mom had found a vegan organic co-op in Brooklyn and had stocked up on enough spelt and granola to last until the triplets went to college. Luckily, Avery had used Edie's credit card to place a FreshDirect order. Now the cabinets were weirdly schizophrenic: there was brown cardboard–wrapped spelt alongside tins of smoked oysters, Carr water crackers, and every variety of Pepperidge Farm cookies known to man. She pulled out a package of mint Milano cookies from the cupboard and walked out onto the terrace. She needed sugar.

'How's the bitch brigade?' Baby lay on the hammock she'd set up on the terrace as soon as they moved in. Sometimes she even slept out there. She was still wearing her Constance skirt, but with a paper-thin C&C California tank Avery recognized from her own closet and an armful of chunky bracelets. Baby looked cool without trying, which was completely unfair, because if there was anything that was a constant in Avery's life, it was that she always had to work for everything: her looks, her grades, her popularity. But even though Baby was beautiful, she was never bitchy about it. If anything, she almost treated her appearance – and the inevitable reactions of people around her – as a minor annoyance. It wasn't anything special, it just *was*.

Hmm, how existential. So if she's beautiful but no one is there to see it, does her beauty still exist?

'So?' Baby prompted. 'How was jamming with the oldies?'

'It was . . . interesting,' Avery hesitated. She didn't want to tell Baby how much the meetings sucked. Baby would just think it was hilarious, and that would depress the hell out of Avery. And unfortunately, it wasn't like she could quit the position. That would be a complete black mark on her Constance record. 'How are *you*? I feel like I haven't seen you in forever. Move over.' Avery pushed Baby's thin, tanned legs off the hammock so she could sit next to her. She gazed at the pinkish-orange sun setting over Central Park and beyond. Ever since they moved to New York, the two sisters just didn't talk as much. Baby was always busy with J.P., and Avery was still bitter that she'd almost gotten *arrested* trying to help her brother and sister get acquainted with their peers here in New York. Not only had Baby skipped the party, now she was running around with Jack's old boyfriend. Why did Baby have to go and get herself a boyfriend – someone *else's* boyfriend – and make things so complicated? Especially now, when Jack and Avery were becoming friends.

'Good. I think I might head over to J.P.'s in a few. I don't really know what we're doing, but I've been busy with *Rancor* stuff, so I haven't really seen him too much this week. I kind of feel bad.' Baby blinked her large brown eyes lazily at her sister.

'You know, maybe for a while it'd be better if you and J.P. weren't so *obvious*. Like, maybe he shouldn't pick you up after school. I feel like that's kind of rubbing it in Jack's face.' Avery savagely dug her fingers into the bag of Milanos. She was starving for junky, un-delicate, not-tea-party food.

'I don't think it matters. She knows I'm dating J.P., so it's not some big secret,' Baby remarked. Had Avery forgotten how much of a huge bitch Jack had been to them both? Besides, she hadn't *stolen* J.P. at all, things had just . . . happened. 'You don't understand.' Baby pushed Avery with her tiny yet surprisingly strong legs off the hammock.

'What do you mean I don't understand?' Avery asked coldly, standing up. She hated the way Baby invoked her holier-than-thou voice, just because she'd had long-term relationships and Avery . . . well, hadn't. She was a little self-conscious about that blip in her personal history. Somehow, nothing ever quite worked out between her and boys. The first time she'd made out with a guy, in eighth grade, on a school trip to Boston, she'd ended up accidentally knocking out his front tooth. It had been totally humiliating and a story that had followed her into high school. Luckily, no one had to know about that here. In New York, it'd all be different. Here in New York, anything was possible.

Especially love.

She plunked down on the ground beside the hammock and hugged her knees to her chest. The bag of cookies was already half empty. Scones were *so* last millennium.

'I'm sorry. I don't think me and J.P. getting together was wrong. Sometimes relationships just *happen*. But it's hard to explain to you, because you're happy on your own. You're . . . ' Baby paused, searching for the right metaphor. 'You're sort of like a panda.' Baby sounded so much like their mom that Avery wanted to scream.

'And you're like an idiot. Point?' Avery said coldly. A panda? What the fuck did that mean? This was supposed to be a sisterly bonding moment. Now she just wanted to go right back out the door and hang out with Jack and Genevieve and Jiffy and anyone else *normal*. Maybe tonight they could raid each other's closets, dress up in ridiculously fabulous Valentino gowns, and go out dancing until the wee hours at some cool new Meatpacking District club. That was what she'd always imagined New York life would be like. But so far, they'd either hung out on the steps of the Met or at Jiffy's cavernous apartment.

'It's not bad to be a panda!' Baby giggled and flipped onto her back again, like some sort of bipolar trout. 'They're super independent, just like you. You know what you want and don't let guys get in the way. I'm more like a . . . ' Baby paused, considering.

'Lobster?' Avery suggested mutinously.

'Mate for life? I don't know. Maybe, I guess.' Baby nodded cheerily and giggled. Somehow, the tension melted and Avery smiled at her tiny, philosophical sister.

Baby giggled and grabbed three cookies. Despite her penchant for all-natural products, Baby had a huge sweet tooth and could easily down an entire package of cookies if she wanted to. Without gaining any weight.

Don't hate her because she's a skinny pig.

'Oh man, what a day,' Owen groaned. He walked out

onto the terrace, wearing wrinkled A&F cargo shorts and no shirt. He looked sunburned, and his typically easygoing expression seemed worried and tense. His sisters eyed him sympathetically.

Baby handed him the Milanos. When they were younger they used to have speed eating competitions, which Baby usually won. Baby smiled, remembering. Life had been so *simple* back then. 'What's up? Exhausted by your entourage?' she teased, making room for him on the hammock. Owen ignored the free space and pretended to sit on top of her.

'Owen, stop!' Baby squealed. Avery smiled. It was nice, just being out here, the three of them, away from old ladies and mean Constance girls and cheating boyfriends.

I'm sure he feels the same way. Especially about the boyfriends part.

'My entourage . . .' Owen trailed off.

'All the girls following you around, silly. But seriously, have you hooked up with anyone? Because, you know, Jiffy really likes you and she's growing her bangs out,' Avery said.

'I haven't hooked up with anyone,' Owen lied. He hadn't told them about Kelsey. First, because it had just seemed so *skanky* to have sex with a random girl on the beach. Then, when he got to New York, everything was just so complicated, and now it was hard even to know where to begin. He wasn't sure if he should tell them about the whole gay thing, or if they'd just make fun of him.

Right, because what sibling would ever do that?

Just then, Edie walked out onto the terrace, two Buddhist chimes dangling from her wrists. 'Helloooo, my darlings!' she exclaimed, sweeping in to kiss each of her children. 'What are we talking about?'

'Nothing,' all three said at the same time.

Edie sat on the hammock and clinked the ancient-looking brass chimes together loudly. 'You know, things are going so well for you all.' She looked at her brood like a proud mother hen. 'I was just thinking – what if we have a dinner party? You can bring your friends, and I'll bring mine. It'll be fantastic!'

Avery nodded tightly. She loved her hippietastic mom but wasn't quite sure she was ready to introduce her Constance friends to her.

'How about next Friday? I really want to make this apartment feel like a home. Maybe we could all do some sort of collaborative art project!' Edie mused, clinking the chimes together again as she stood up and floated back inside. Owen shrugged, and Baby rolled her eyes happily, but Avery felt a cold knot of fear in her stomach.

Come, now. Everyone loves a party.

notes from the underground

Baby and Sydney giggled breathlessly in a cab headed to the Lower East Side on Friday evening. They'd just come from their latest adventure with Underground Response, at the Union Square Whole Foods, where the group's mission had been to act like groupies for various cashiers. Baby was wearing a black slip she'd found in Avery's closet, fishnets, and Christian Louboutin ankle boots that were sure to provoke Avery's wrath once she realized they were missing. All together, Baby looked very 1920s-flapper-meets-dominatrix.

Meow.

'We're getting out,' Sydney commanded as the cab screeched to a halt on Houston Street. Baby climbed out of the cab and onto the dirty sidewalk, feeling a tiny bit guilty for blowing off J.P. tonight. Last night they'd hung out, taking his dogs for a walk and then watching a movie in the Cashmans' massive screening room, but they hadn't gone out-out since they'd officially become a couple. He'd wanted to go and see some French film that had gotten rave reviews in *The New Yorker*. Normally, Baby liked random, obscure movies, but she had the feeling he'd only suggested it to try to make her happy. Besides, she reminded herself, she *had* to do the *Rancor* stuff just to be allowed to even *stay* at Constance.

Together, Baby and Sydney ran down the street and zigzagged along the uneven side-street blocks, passing metal-grated storefronts that seemed out of place next to their velvet-rope club neighbors. The Lower East Side had been one of Baby's biggest disappointments when she'd moved to New York a month ago. She had expected it to be all urban and gritty, but instead it was filled with trying-too-hard bars that did their best to look divey inside but had velvet ropes and photographers outside, just like everywhere else.

'I don't know if I want to go out . . .' Baby began. Maybe she should just go back to J.P. She'd rather just hang out with him than go to some hot, uncomfortable bar.

But Sydney didn't seem to hear her. She marched into a dirty takeout restaurant. SUPAR MEXICAN, CHINESE, AND SUSHI! was written on a large cardboard sign propped in the window.

Sounds, um, supar.

'I told Webber we'd meet him here, okay?' Sydney raised her eyebrows excitedly.

'I'm not really hungry . . .' Baby trailed off as they walked into the tiny, dingy takeout joint. A grubby laminated menu was perched on the cracked Formica counter. One guy stood behind the counter stirring a pot of an unidentified brown substance, his unibrow furrowed in consternation. Baby was all for no pretension, but she drew the line at mystery meat.

'I'll go first – you follow, okay?' Sydney trailed off mysteriously as she entered what looked like a broom closet.

Figuring she had nothing to lose, Baby followed. Instead, they found themselves in an outdoor alley.

What was she expecting, Oz? Narnia?

Sydney scanned the empty alley and authoritatively marched up to an industrial-size metal door. She knocked three times. Baby nervously stood behind her. Was this some type of cult initiation or something?

The door opened, and a small girl wearing all black held out a clipboard.

'Name?' she asked.

'Here for Webber,' Sydney said confidently. The girl opened the door, and suddenly, they were transported to a cavernous, wood-paneled, underground bar. Baby breathed out in surprise. A secret bar? How cool! *This* was the type of New York she'd expected. Vintage propagandist type posters from KGB-era Russia were tacked on the wall, and a DJ in the corner was spinning bhangra trance music. Baby felt like she had just stepped into some 1920s speakeasy, or an intellectual dissident bar in Communist Russia.

You know, either one.

'Isn't this awesome?' Sydney murmured, scanning the crowd for Webber. She stood on tiptoe in her Doc Martens. The bar was crowded, but not with any of the khaki-wearing, button-down losers who usually ran around like they owned New York.

Losers except for her khaki-pants-and-button-down-wearing boyfriend, of course.

'Sexy bitch!' Webber sneaked up behind Sydney and bit her neck lightly. Baby looked away. It was weird watching a guy named Webber make out with her friend.

'Hey lover.' Sydney kissed him and suddenly Baby felt

left out. She wandered over to the bar, away from the Underground Response crowd. A cloud of smoke wafted over her and, for the first time, she wanted a cigarette. She wasn't really a smoker of anything. Although she'd smoked a little pot back in Nantucket, she preferred to keep her lungs clean. Now, though, she wanted to inhale the city in all its carcinogenic glory.

She plunked down on a tall wooden stool. The guy next to her was tall and skinny, with curly brown hair and a sky blue T-shirt with some slogan written in Spanish. She vaguely remembered him from the Whole Foods event, where he'd eagerly spent the whole time squeezing the melons in the produce section before handing them out to customers. He was drinking a large glass of what looked like water and gazing up at the handwritten list of beers above the bar.

'Hey, can I have one?' she asked boldly, indicating the pack of cigarettes lying near him on top of the slick bar.

'Sure.' He studied her face and Baby smiled. 'I noticed you before,' he said shyly. He pulled out a cigarette, put it in his mouth, and lit it, unleashing a thin stream of pink smoke.

'Sobranies,' he explained as he offered it to her. 'They're from Russia. I use them to impress the ladies,' he said wryly. Baby glanced at him, unsure if he was making fun of her. 'Unless you'd like something stronger?'

Baby shook her head. After dating one raging stoner, she had no desire to repeat *that* experience anytime soon.

'Good.' He smiled and picked up his glass. 'What's your name?' he asked, with a slight hint of a Spanish accent, like he had just stepped off a yacht in the Maldives.

'Baby.' She smiled at him and held out her tiny hand. It was so cool to finally meet more people.

How friendly!

'That's beautiful.' He cupped her tiny chin and locked his tequila-colored eyes with hers. It was a gesture that made Baby feel like she was a racehorse being appraised. She pulled her face away and took a long drag of the cigarette, then started coughing. 'Fuck!' She choked, grabbing his glass. She drank from it, sputtering.

'This is all vodka!' she exclaimed, and tried to wipe the drool off her chin as he clapped her back.

'You are okay?' he asked, as if answering his own question. Baby nodded, taking another, slower, sip of vodka. She breathed carefully.

'I'm Mateo,' he said. 'From Barcelona. Have you been there?'

'No.' Baby looked around to see where the rest of the UR group was. Most were crammed in a corner, drinking beer out of pitchers and playing some type of drinking game that involved articles of clothing being taken off, traded, and repurposed. Sydney's slip was wrapped artfully around one guy's head like a turban, and Sydney and Webber were now making out in the corner.

'I've never been to Barcelona,' Baby clarified, blowing pink smoke upward to the industrial, steel roof. He was probably in college, she guessed. Despite her hippie-bohemianism, she had really never traveled very much, except for the one time she and Avery had gone to Paris for a week with Grandmother Avery as a thirteenth birthday present. Baby had spent her time accidentally-on-purpose trying to get lost in the artsy neighborhoods of Montmartre, while Avery and Grandmother Avery had spent afternoons shopping at Chanel and Givenchy and drinking kir royales at overpriced cafés along the Seine.

'You should come. You would love it. You look like a girl who needs an adventure.' He grinned, then pulled out a silver Zippo lighter and flicked it to light his own cigarette. 'Cheers to adventures!' he said, awkwardly bumping their cigarettes together.

'Why are you here?' Baby asked curiously, taking another sip of his vodka.

'The wind brought me here.' He smiled.

'Do you know how lame that sounds in English?' Baby rolled her eyes.

'No, it's true. My friend, Fernando, and I came here. We needed a change.'

Baby arched a dark eyebrow, intrigued, and took another sip of his vodka.

'Would be easier to have your own drink, no?' Mateo teased and expertly gestured to the bartender, who filled a large tumbler with vodka and set it in front of Baby.

'We made a pact,' Mateo continued. 'Anytime, day or night, one of us would call. We would meet at the airport, passport, toothbrushes, then take the first flight here. We called it "doing the New York." I called him last week and we've been here ever since. Fun city.' Mateo grinned.

'Where are you staying?' Baby asked, impressed. Show up at the airport at the drop of a hat, with only a toothbrush? That sounded so *cool*.

'We stay at a hostel. With friends. We make friends.' He chuckled. 'So, Baby, what's your story?'

'I live here.' Baby shrugged. Suddenly, her life didn't seem very exciting. She racked her brain trying to think of something to say that wouldn't make her sound like a dumb high school girl. It was weird – usually she wasn't at a loss for words, but Mateo's sexy Spanish accent was distracting.

'I'm always looking for adventures too,' she finally offered, a small smile playing on her lips. She wasn't sure if it was the vodka or the pink cigarettes, but she just felt at home. Just then, her cell rang loudly from her vintage Chanel bag, also courtesy of Avery's closet.

'Your boyfriend?' Mateo asked, nodding toward her bag. Baby frowned, then picked up.

'Hey gorgeous, where are you?' J.P.'s voice asked. Baby stiffened and turned away from Mateo. She looked down at her knees, smoothing her slip over her bare skin self-consciously. She hated how he always greeted her by calling her *gorgeous* or *beautiful*. She knew most girls would love it, but for her, it felt like J.P. was saying it because he *had* to. In a weird way, it sounded scripted.

'Just . . . working on *Rancor* stuff,' she said, pressing her ear closer to the phone and hoping he couldn't hear the raucous noise in the background. 'Actually, we're at a bar photographing something for *Rancor*,' she clarified, just in case he could.

'Okay, you're still there? It sounds like you're in a construction zone or something.' J.P. chuckled. 'Anyway, are you done soon?' he asked hopefully. 'I could make reservations at Orsay. The chef's really into the organic movement. I thought you'd like that,' he offered.

Baby recognized the name of one of the overpriced restaurants in their neighborhood. Sitting in some stuffy restaurant and hearing the server explain the life of her dinner was the last thing she wanted to do right now.

'Actually, Sydney and I need to finish some stuff up,' she lied. 'But you should come with us next time. We're profiling this crazy improv group,' she elaborated, feeling even more guilty than she had before.

But not guilty enough to *leave* . . .

'You're the boss!' J.P. said agreeably. 'I'll miss you tonight, gorgeous.'

Mwah! Mwah!

'See, you do have a boyfriend,' Mateo said teasingly after Baby hung up. He put his hand close to Baby's.

'I go with the wind,' Baby said mysteriously, wrinkling her nose at him. She wasn't flirting, she reasoned. She was doing research!

And we all know cute foreign boys make the most interesting subjects.

the queen

On Monday afternoon, Jack slammed her Givenchy satchel down at the round table in the Constance Billard cafeteria and dug into the 2 percent strained Greek organic yogurt she'd bought at the grimy bodega all the way over on Second Avenue. Her yogurt had cost a fucktastic five dollars. They'd also had a freaking surprise essay in English this morning, which was not ideal considering Jack hadn't done any of the reading this past weekend. She'd only managed to pull some vague thoughts together about *Moby-Dick*, which was just a stupid title for an even dumber book about fucking whales. At least she hoped it was mostly about whales, since that's what she'd written about. But, in any case, her essay sucked, meaning she'd have to go and have a talk with her nosebleed-prone guidance counselor, Ms Glos, and either tell her she was emotionally exhausted or that she hadn't read the book because the violent descriptions of whale harpooning offended her. She hadn't decided which yet.

'Hey.' Jiffy came up behind her and sat down, shoving her way-too-long bangs out of her brown eyes. Her tray was laden with russet potato fries, and their grease reflected the soft light of the cafeteria's dimmed lights. Jack's stomach grumbled loudly and she sighed in annoyance. Why couldn't she be one of those girls who lost her appetite when she got stressed out? She greedily grabbed two fries.

Jiffy wordlessly passed the entire plate to Jack with her Chanel Midnight Satin–manicured hand. Midnight Satin was so last season, but Jiffy was the type of girl who held on to trends until they died. Since her parents were on the board of practically every philanthropic organization in New York and her thirty-two-year-old sister was one of the most sought-after socialites on the party scene, she could kind of get away with it.

'You can have the rest – I'm not that hungry,' Jiffy offered with a slight hint of a sigh.

Genevieve and Sarah Jane walked over and sat down. Genevieve yawned loudly. 'Something needs to happen,' she announced.

'There's that St Jude's party coming up,' Jiffy suggested cheerfully, eyeing Jack's French fry consumption like a hawk. Since she'd grown up as almost an only child, she tended to be a little possessive. 'My sister thinks it'll get a lot of attention from the media.' Jiffy's eyes gleamed. 'Maybe we could go to Barneys and look for outfits? Or maybe Bergdorf's?'

Suddenly Jiffy jumped, making a pained face like she'd been kicked. 'Ow!' she whined to Genevieve. She looked over at Jack guiltily. 'Um, I don't need anything, actually. Maybe we could just . . . hang out after school?' she finished lamely.

'Or, if *you* need something, Jack, we could always run to the fashion closet at *Bella*,' Sarah Jane offered, naming the major fashion glossy that her mom edited. 'No one would notice. If they did, it'd just be blamed on some assistant.' Sarah Jane shrugged, taking her black-rimmed Prada glasses off and inspecting them.

What? Jack's eyes narrowed. Since when did Sarah Jane offer up fashion closet privileges? Jack glanced over at Genevieve, who suddenly seemed extremely preoccupied with her reflection in one of the cafeteria's mirrored walls.

And then it hit her: Genevieve must have told everybody that Jack was a destitute loser. *Bitch*, Jack thought furiously.

'Thanks,' Jack said, her voice dripping with sarcasm. She looked around the table, but no one would make eye contact. Sarah Jane grabbed her yogurt cup, reading the nutrition label while Jiffy idly played with a fry. Now they wouldn't even look at her? She randomly thought of *Moby-Dick*. Maybe getting on a boat and going to the middle of the ocean wasn't such a bad idea. She'd get so tan and skinny that everyone would be way jealous, even if she was a poor loser. 'Thanks a lot, Genevieve. I can't believe you told them.'

'Jack, you're freaking. I just thought they should know. Seriously, there's no need for this *drama*.' Genevieve sighed in exasperation. 'If I wanted drama, I'd just go to LA and hang out at Les Deux.' Genevieve took every opportunity to bitch about LA, but it inevitably made her sound like Joan Crawford or some other million-year-old actress bemoaning the demise of Old Hollywood.

'Besides, I *am* sick of Barneys,' Jiffy offered lamely, smiling slightly. Jack felt herself soften.

'Yeah, right.' Sarah Jane snorted in disbelief.

'It's true!' Jiffy bleated, examining her hair for nonexistent split ends. 'We're your friends, right?' Jiffy asked Jack. It was a genuine question, and Jack smiled. They still liked her. They cared about her. They wanted to be her friend, musty garret and all.

'Thanks, guys.' Jack sighed. 'It's only temporary.' She felt a lump in her throat. *Fuck.* It was one thing to be poor, but to start *crying*? *That* would really ruin her reputation.

'Hey guys!' Avery Carlyle chirped behind them. Jack whirled around. Avery's hair was in a high ponytail and held back with a mirrored Stella McCartney headband. She wore a pretty pink Tocca blouse Jack had seen the last time she was in Barneys. Avery set down her stainless steel tray and took the seat right next to Jack. 'I can't believe that's all you're eating!' she exclaimed, gesturing to Jack's yogurt. She glanced down at her extra-large salad. 'I feel like *such* a pig today. So, what's up for later? Want to do a Barneys run?' Avery asked, looking around at the girls. She couldn't wait to get their opinions on dresses for the St Jude's benefit. It was so *cute* how Owen would be auctioned off, and she couldn't *wait* to see the other swim team guys. Besides, it seemed so classic New York to get ready for a benefit.

Jack smiled at Avery's perky expression. Avery might have been able to blackmail her into being friends, but now that the secret was out, so was Avery. Out of her life, out of her friends' lives, and hopefully, before long, she'd want to be completely out of New York. *Perfect.* Jack wheeled around so that she was facing Avery. She'd been waiting to do this for far too long.

'Actually, Avery, it's such a coincidence you brought up Barneys, because we were just talking about it. Turns out, no one wants to go. Especially not with you.' She was impressed with the way she sounded: apologetic, with an undercurrent of complete bitchiness.

'Excuse me?' Avery stared at her with one eyebrow raised, a slight warning tone in her voice. Most people would hear that undercurrent and take back whatever they said. But most people weren't Jack Laurent.

'You're fun, don't get me wrong. Remember how much fun it was when the cops came to your party?' Jack laughed in Avery's face. Avery's silvery blue eyes changed in an instant from defensive to confused to devastated. Across the table, Jack registered a flicker of concern in Jiffy's eyes. Well, so what? She was just giving Avery, the blackmailing bitch, *exactly* what she deserved.

'What's going on?' Avery asked, looking at Jiffy. Jiffy sometimes seemed kind of dumb, but she was definitely the friendliest of the group, and right now Avery felt like she needed a friend. Her stomach was in a thirty-story free fall.

'Oh my God, could you just drop the innocent thing for once?' Jack exploded angrily. All the rage and frustration she'd held in for the past two weeks – toward her stingy, lame dad, her ridiculous mom, the absurd family that had moved into *her* house, and her dumb-ass boyfriend who'd dumped her – was ready to spill out. She took a deep breath, trying to control the rush of emotion. This was *her* moment to reclaim her rightful place as queen of the junior class, and she had to be in control. Several tables over, a group of ninth graders looked up. Jack glared at them and definitively stood up. She might as well give a performance to remember. Maybe the younger Constance girls could learn from her. Especially since they certainly wouldn't learn anything from Avery, their SLBO or SLOB or whatever the fuck that position was called. 'I was the one who called the cops on your party. Just thought you should know,' Jack said, enunciating each word. 'We're not really your friends, and nobody likes you.' She shrugged for the benefit of the rest of the cafeteria, then sat back down.

Show's over!

Avery pushed her chair back so fast it clattered to the floor. She knew her face was bright red and her chest was probably breaking out in the unfortunate hives that only appeared when she was about to cry.

'No wonder your boyfriend dumped you for my sister,' she hissed loudly. She didn't bother to pick up the over-turned chair or even look at any of those bitches. She stifled a sigh as she marched past the sea of now familiar faces, sixtysomething pairs of eyes boring into her back. She marched into the Constance ladies' room and only then, in the handicapped last stall usually reserved for girls having secret emotional breakdowns, did she allow herself to cry.

'Thank God we don't have to hang out with *her* anymore.' Jack breathed a sigh of relief. Maybe they *should* take a look at the *Bella* fashion closet this afternoon. Then she noticed Jiffy shaking her head wistfully.

'What?' Jack snapped in exasperation.

'She has a hot brother . . .' Jiffy trailed off. Sarah Jane nodded in affirmation.

'He's taken anyway.' Genevieve sighed. 'I told you, all the hot ones are taken. That's why we need to step it up and get some guys back in our lives. We need to figure out our St Jude's benefit party strategy. That's the thing. In

LA, everyone has a party strategy. I think we need to pick it up here,' she announced, as if she were a general dispatching her troops.

'What do you mean, he's taken?' Jiffy asked, completely ignoring Genevieve's stupid idea.

A party strategy sounded exactly like something Avery Carlyle would have, Jack thought darkly. Then, immediately, she perked up. She didn't have to worry about Avery anymore. She was back on top. She had her friends. She'd have ballet, once she got that scholarship. Her life was almost back to normal.

Except for her self-proclaimed destitution and her recent public dumpage?

'I saw him with that blond, artsy Seaton Arms girl, after Avery's party. They were talking outside his building while I was on my way home. They looked like they were, like, about to do it right there in front of the doorman,' Genevieve said importantly, clearly happy to have unearthed a nugget of gossip that had previously held no value. Jack thought back. She remembered Avery's brother from the party. He had the same blond hair as his sister, and except for a ridiculous half-beard, he'd been pretty hot, in an outdoorsy, skater/snowboarder/swimmer boy type of way.

'Well, he couldn't have been, since she's with that swimmer dude from St Jude's. Rhys Sterling? My mom *hates* his mother,' Sarah Jane burst in. 'Her name's Kelsey something. We went to riding camp together in seventh grade. But she and Rhys have been together forever. Remember, they totally hooked up at Genevieve's bat mitzvah?' Genevieve's father had rented out Radio City Music Hall and hired U2 to perform. Jack vaguely remembered Rhys and his girlfriend holding hands and sneaking kisses back then. That was the thing. Even though Upper East Siders were spread among five or six private schools, everybody knew one another through a complex social network of families. Everyone knew everything about everybody, so it made it extra hard to hide.

'You're probably just confused, Genevieve. You *were* a little drunk at Avery's party,' Sarah Jane said puritanically. She stole a fry off Jiffy's plate.

Like she wasn't Ms Vodka Gimlet?

Jiffy, Sarah Jane, and Genevieve began to chat about the St Jude's swim team guys to determine who was single, but Jack was only half listening. Had Owen really been having a thing with Kelsey? But Kelsey and Rhys were together. And Owen and Rhys were best friends. If Genevieve really *had* seen them together, then there was something seriously fishy going on. *Interesting.*

Jack swung her Givenchy satchel over her shoulder, a plan forming in her head. 'I have to jet,' she said breezily to the group, and waltzed out the cafeteria's double doors. If blackmail was the Carlyles' way, then maybe they deserved a taste of their own medicine.

Ding-dong, the bitch is back!

gossipgirl.net

Disclaimer: All the real names of places, people, and events have been altered or abbreviated to protect the innocent. Namely, me.

topics   sightings   your e-mail   post a question

hey people!

a little intrigue is good for the reputation

Every rule has its exception, and sometimes the more you learn about someone, the more mysterious they become. Take, for example, one Upper East Side princess who was recently downgraded from the lap of luxury. She thought it was a shameful secret, but do we really *care* either way? Instead of her fairy-tale castle, she's living in an attic of cast-off antiques – which, for my money, is far more romantic than living in some tacky penthouse.

Besides, it finally lends some credibility to her artistic persona. Look at Isadora Duncan, Zelda Fitzgerald, Edna St Vincent Millay. Colette. Did they come from money? Who knows? Who cares? They were total icons, ahead of their times. Which, as we all know, has no price tag – despite what some think. (I'm looking at you Black AmEx holders who are desperately trying to buy taste, one Diane von Furstenberg wrap dress at a time. You know who you are!) Point being: little princess, fear not. Nobody's pitying you. The one person who *is* receiving widespread pity right now didn't lose her money – she lost her so-called friends and her social standing. And what's sadder than that?

sightings

J stopping a scrawny guy with a Speedo over his khakis, asking what time St Jude's gets out for lunch. Does someone have a secret crush? Or a Speedo fetish . . .? **A** in the headmistress's office, eating small cucumber sandwiches with a blue-haired lady and Mrs M, discussing *Eat, Pray, Love.* Hey, I've heard book clubs are good ways to make new friends. Especially when you don't have any your age . . . **B** and **J.P.** at a not-open-to-the-public wine tasting at the **Cashman Lofts**' unnamed organic-only bar. **B** again, outside Cashman Lofts with **S**, frolicking in the fountain with some scruffy guys and taking pictures. Hmm, it's been a while since a **B** and an **S** were spotted together. Guess it really is a new era!

your e-mail

Q: Dearest Woman of the Rumors,

I am student from Spain. My boyfriend, who is Spanish royalty and a big prize here, seems to have run off to New York. Do you know him? Please to send him back to me. His mother is looking for him!!!

– Caliente Chica

A: Dear CC,

One question: Is he cute? If so, I'll keep my eyes peeled!

– GG

Q: Dear Gossip Girl,

I work at a very busy and important magazine, and I think some people just came in and took stuff from the fashion closet. I'm just an assistant, and I'm totally freaking the fuck out. If anyone is reading this, please return what you took, no questions asked.

– SlaveToFashion

A: Dear STF,

Um, this isn't the lost and found. Sorry.

– GG

Q: Dear Gossip Girl,

I heard that **A** is actually, like, Mrs M's spy. She's really twenty-five and has a PhD from Princeton, and she was going to work for the FBI, but then Mrs M got her first. Is that true?

– Freeek

A: Dear Freeek,

A is certainly sophisticated, but something tells me she's not quite FBI material. Still, it doesn't hurt to be careful what you're saying or doing. In this town, someone's always watching.

– GG

Okay, just two short weeks left till the St Jude's swim team benefit. And, as we all know, it's not who you're bidding on but who you're going home with that really counts. Luckily, some anonymous benefactor donated a whole block of rooms at the **Delancey**, the brand-new Lower East Side hotel where the benefit's taking place, to the cause. Talk about an easy commute. Hope all you single ladies are saving your pennies!

You know you love me,

Gossip
Girl

maybe girlfriends do grow on trees. . . .

Owen Carlyle stepped into the pizza place on the corner of Eighty-eighth and First during lunch on Tuesday, relieved to be away from St Jude's even for a few moments. Since the first bell had rung on Monday, he'd been continually bombarded with references to his supposed homosexuality, enduring, among other things, a discussion about homoerotic overtones in *Othello* in English class and a lecture by Ms Kendall in art history about the male gaze in Renaissance portraiture. Everyone had looked to him for his input, as if he were this gay expert or something. Whatever. Owen shrugged it off as he inhaled the warm, yeasty scent of rising dough.

'My man, what do you want?' The beefy pizza guy behind the counter smiled jovially.

'Two sausages.' Owen cringed when he realized how his order could be interpreted. 'Er, two slices of sausage,' he amended. 'Warmed up, please.' His eyes landed on the thick gold chain nestled in the pizza guy's fuzzy chest hair. Yuck. If Owen needed proof he wasn't gay, that was it.

'Nice day, huh, buddy?' the pizza guy asked affably as he leaned his thick, hamlike arms across the glass counter. He looked like he was ready to settle in for an all-day chat. Owen nodded tersely.

'You go to that fancy school?' the guy questioned, his eyes flicking over Owen's blazer. Owen nodded, wishing he hadn't asked for the slices to be warmed up, so he could just get the hell out of here. This wasn't the usual guy. Maybe it was the owner or something. It seemed like a pretty good life, Owen thought. Maybe he should just open up a pizza place and forget about girls, school, and swimming. He'd make people happy. It wouldn't be so bad.

Just then, the bell on the door rang. Owen whirled around to see Hugh Moore. Fabulous.

'Two sausages!' the pizza guy crowed. He pulled the steaming slices out of the oven and slid them onto a white paper plate and over to Owen.

'Thanks,' Owen muttered.

'Woooah.' Hugh took a few steps back and widened his eyes crazily. 'Hey, slugger. Way to go for the sausage! Didn't mean to interrupt anything!' Hugh grinned devilishly as he sauntered out the door. Owen tried to keep his cool. He could feel the tips of his ears turn bright red.

'You want some spice?' the pizza guy asked, indicating the green plastic tray of oregano and pepper flake containers.

'No!' Owen practically backed away. Ever since people started thinking he was gay, he was finding sexual allusions *everywhere*. It was a bit like when he first moved to New York, when anything and everything would remind him of Kat.

Even hairy pizza guys?

'I mean, I'll just take these to go.' He threw a ten on the counter. 'Keep the change,' he muttered. He stuffed the larger slice in his mouth as he exited onto the street. The slice burned the roof of his mouth and the cheese was soggy and tasteless. He threw the plate in a metal trash can.

'Owen, right?'

Owen looked over and saw a pretty, auburn-haired girl wearing the same uniform that Baby and Avery wore to school. She looked like a gazelle, or like one of the dancers in the Degas painting that hung in the study in Grandmother Avery's house. He wondered how she knew him. He didn't really remember seeing her at Avery's party, but then again, he'd been a little bit preoccupied.

It takes *so* much concentration to orchestrate an imaginary breakup with your best friend's girlfriend.

'Yeah,' Owen mumbled. He looked around in case this was some bizarre swim team prank, but the only person in sight was an elderly lady driving a motorized wheelchair down the street, chased by her three sweater-clad Yorkies.

'Jack Laurent.' She smiled and held out her hand.

Owen took it, then dropped it as if he'd been burned. Girls were too much trouble. He couldn't do this. 'Nice to meet you,' he said awkwardly. Her pink-glossed lips turned into a frown at his less-than-warm greeting. Owen recognized that expression as classic girl, meant to soften him. And Jack was gorgeous. But he wasn't going to fall for that. He would remain stoic.

And gay.

'Sorry, I wish I had more time to talk.' He shrugged helplessly. 'I'm just in a rush.' He turned to the crosswalk.

The sign blinked DON'T WALK, and cars were already streaming up the avenue. He stared straight ahead, determined not to look at her.

'Oh, okay,' Jack said softly. She eyed him critically. He was cuter than she had anticipated, with broad, athletic shoulders and a trim waist. His blue eyes reminded her of the disastrous Saint-Tropez vacation she'd gone on with her mother a few years ago, when her mother had fallen in love with some native who'd almost convinced her to move there. Owen loosened his maroon tie, still not looking at her. He was nervous, Jack realized. She decided to give him something to *really* be nervous about. 'Are you running back to meet Kelsey?' she asked innocently.

It worked. The tips of his ears turned bright red against his blond hair. Jack smiled as if she were really a concerned citizen, just interested in current affairs.

'Kelsey?' Owen choked. He could almost feel the lump of pizza he'd just eaten coming back up.

'Isn't that your girlfriend?' Jack widened her green eyes.

They were still standing on the corner, and suddenly Owen felt very exposed. He looked inside the pizza place. The pizza guy was by himself, bopping up and down to some song. The cars had stopped, and the WALK sign was on.

'Let's walk,' Owen instructed. He couldn't *believe* he'd been discovered. There really were spies everywhere. No wonder Avery was always so paranoid. They reached Eighty-seventh between First and York. 'First of all, she's not my girlfriend. I barely know her, except that she used to date my buddy, Rhys,' Owen announced.

'Are you sure?' Jack demanded. It was kind of fun doing

this. She felt like a sexy girl spy, like Anne Hathaway from that totally dumb movie, *Get Smart*.

'Why do you care?' Owen asked point-blank. His voice rose. He'd had *enough* of everyone scrutinizing him.

'Because I need a favor.' Jack dropped the spy tack in favor of a more demure, sex-kitten-with-a-heart-of-gold persona, sort of like Marilyn Monroe in *Bus Stop*, an old movie she and J.P. had once watched in his screening room. She'd had the idea the instant she realized Owen might have a secret: she had nothing to lose by pretending she knew about a Kelsey/Owen tryst. If they *had* been together, then Owen would have to do pretty much anything she asked to keep her from spreading the rumor. Why not have a little fun with him? She could totally drive Avery and Baby crazy in the process.

'My boyfriend broke up with me last week. I haven't been able to sleep, I haven't been able to eat – I just feel so ugly,' Jack continued, really getting into it. It felt good to tell *someone* how shitty and out of control she felt lately. And Owen actually seemed like he was listening. He'd fallen into step with her and was nodding like he really *cared* about what she had to say.

'You're so hot, and every girl on the Upper East Side wants you. But I know that something happened with you and Kelsey and you have to keep it a secret. I don't want to blackmail you . . .' She batted her eyelashes and smiled. She was skipping English right now, and she *still* hadn't even cracked open *Moby*-fucking-*Dick*.

Who needs literature when you're the mistress of dark subplots?

'What do you want from me?' Owen narrowed his eyes at her. She looked so innocent and vulnerable and beautiful that he momentarily softened. He *did* know firsthand how much breakups sucked.

'Could you pretend to be my boyfriend?'

'What?' Owen demanded in case he'd misheard. He knew girls were weird, but this seemed absurd. Even Avery wouldn't ask a guy to do that.

They were nearing East End Avenue and Owen noticed a group of St Jude's guys across the street. They turned and stared silently. *Great.* Every guy in his school thought he batted for the other team. He looked at Jack, whose beautiful green eyes pleaded. They almost reminded him of his golden retriever, Chance, when he really wanted a walk. Not that he was comparing her to a dog or anything.

What do you call a female dog again?

The St Jude's guys elbowed one another as Jack and Owen walked past, and suddenly Owen had a flash of inspiration. If he went along with her plan, at least no one would think he was gay. In fact, having an insta-girlfriend might not be such a bad idea.

'Um, I have to go to class,' Owen said, evading the question. 'Can we talk more about this later?' He pulled out his iPhone and raised his eyebrows expectantly. 'What's your number?'

Jack grabbed the phone away from him and quickly punched in her phone number. Her hands were cool and Owen felt a jolt of electricity as her fingernails brushed against his palm.

'I understand.' Jack nodded, handing Owen's iPhone back. She looked so guileless as she brushed her auburn hair off her shoulder. But Owen knew from experience that girls always had an ulterior motive. 'So, I'll see you later . . .' She smiled and then kissed him on the cheek.

'Okay.' Owen stepped back involuntarily. What exactly would pretending to be her boyfriend entail?

Lots of benefits!

'Thank you,' she whispered as she walked west, her uniform skirt swirling around her knees. Owen walked up the steps to St Jude's, a smile playing on his face.

Watch out, flipper boy. Playing in the kiddie pool's a far cry from jumping off the deep end . . .

heaven in a handbasket

Rhys lumbered into the Eighty-sixth Street entrance of the park on Tuesday afternoon, weighed down by a custom-packed Dean & DeLuca picnic basket. He'd asked Kelsey to meet him right after her Seaton Arms tennis practice, which conveniently took place at the Central Park tennis courts on Ninety-third. Since she had to walk back home this way anyway, offering to meet her here seemed less stalkerish and desperate and more like they were two old friends catching up. At least he could fall back on that excuse if nothing went according to plan.

But it would, Rhys told himself as he unfolded a Frette sheet on the grassy slope adjacent to the Egyptian wing of the Met. It was beautiful, and it was never too crowded. He nervously pulled out his phone, in case Kelsey was running late.

She wasn't. 'Wow!' Kelsey squealed as she walked up the slope and saw the elaborate spread. In her tennis whites, perky white visor, and white sneakers, she looked like an angel. Her face broke into a wide, sunny grin as she yanked off her shoes and ran across the grass toward him, scattering a collection of pigeons in her path. Rhys sighed in relief. Already this was going better than he'd anticipated.

'Hey!' Kelsey stopped right before she hugged him. Rhys stood up, then sat down on the sheet awkwardly. It was so weird being together, but not *together* together. At least not yet.

Down, boy! Patience is a virtue.

Kelsey sat down next to him and peered inside the picnic basket. She had a small scar on her nose from a nose piercing she'd gotten during a brief moment of rebellion in ninth grade. If you didn't know her, you'd think it was a freckle, but that was the thing – Rhys *did* know her.

Just not as, ahem, *intimately* as some people.

'Oh my God, you brought jelly babies!' She pulled out a yellow package of the British, gummy bear–like candy his dad was obsessed with. 'I love you! I mean . . . I love them,' she trailed off awkwardly as she bit her pale pink bottom lip.

'Yeah, I just pulled together some stuff.' Rhys tried to sound like he hadn't spent the entire weekend racing from Zabar's to Citarella to Dean & DeLuca to prepare the picnic. 'How was practice?' He passed her a water bottle he'd filled with Grey Goose–infused lemonade, her favorite drink.

'Good . . .' Kelsey trailed off. 'You think of everything,' she noted as she took a swig from the container. She leaned back on her elbows, and Rhys stared at her happily. He could have stared at her all day.

'Rhys!' a male voice shouted.

He looked up and saw Hugh Moore, surrounded by Jeff Kohl, Ken Williams, and Ian McDaniel. *Fuck.* Rhys looked down, pretending to be supremely interested in the pattern of the wicker picnic basket, hoping they'd just go away.

'Hey Kelsey, good to see you again. We've missed you.' Hugh winked. 'Might I say, you look lovely tonight.' His eyes lecherously flicked to her tanned upper thighs.

'Thanks,' Kelsey said sweetly. 'How are you? You look really . . . manly with the beard,' she giggled. Rhys smiled tightly.

'I do what I can to impress the ladies.' Hugh shrugged and plopped down next to them. He took a Carr's cracker, smeared it with Brie, and sighed in satisfaction. 'Rhys, Ian's buying you a present right now.' He laughed mischievously. Rhys followed Hugh's line of vision and noticed Ian's skinny frame in front of an ice-cream truck. Oh no. Whatever this was, it wasn't good.

'Rhys wants a Mister Softee!' Hugh yelled loudly. Several people turned to stare. 'I know that's not what *you* need.' Hugh smiled lasciviously at Kelsey as Ian, Hugh, and Ken all lined up and looked down at them, Ian proffering a runny vanilla ice-cream cone.

'No.' Rhys blushed furiously, especially when he saw Kelsey giggling. 'Guys, I'll see you later?' he asked in what he hoped was an authoritative tone. He looked over at Kelsey, hoping she didn't think he was totally gross, or worse, totally lame.

And, you know, a softy.

'Very funny,' she said, laughing. 'You guys want to hang out for a little? There's plenty of food,' Kelsey offered, smiling at the guys. One of the things Rhys loved about Kelsey was she never minded his swim team friends' totally lame jokes or inappropriate senses of humor, but tonight was *not* the night. Rhys held his breath, trying to send a telepathic message to Hugh that he would personally pull his balls off if he stayed.

'No, looks like you've got things to do.' Hugh mercifully stood up. 'Go get 'em, tiger!' he added to Rhys, running down the slope with the guys.

'Sorry about that,' Rhys said desperately. The park was crowded, and people kept stepping over their blanket and peering into their picnic basket, as if they wanted to join in.

'No problem. They're kind of funny. That whole swim team bonding thing, right? That's why you guys haven't shaved? It's cute.' Kelsey reached up and touched the scruff on Rhys's chin with her thumb. 'It's good to see you. Thanks for calling.' She shook her head sadly. 'I didn't think we'd ever talk again.'

'I'd never stop talking to you,' Rhys said simply as he refreshed their Snapple containers. A curious French bulldog wandered over and nosed his way into Rhys's lap. Rhys awkwardly pushed him back and the dog scampered away, leaving a perfect paw imprint in the Brie Rhys had left out. Oh dear. Nothing was going to plan.

Kelsey laughed at the distraught look on his face. 'Don't worry about the cheese. This is so much better than meeting at a restaurant. Really,' she assured him.

Rhys grinned. She knew him, too, how neurotic he got when everything wasn't . . . perfect. 'So, how have you been?' he asked lamely.

Kelsey sighed dramatically. 'Not that good,' she confessed. She bit her blackberry-stained lip and looked off into the distance.

'Really?' Rhys asked, surprised. He hated to think of Kelsey being unhappy, but could it be that she'd been missing him? 'You could have called me. You know, to talk about things. I'm always there for you,' he said gallantly.

Instantly, he began second-guessing himself. Did that sound too timid, too gay-best-friend? He didn't want to be her gay best friend. He wanted to be her very straight, very manly boyfriend.

Kelsey nodded to herself, as if she was deep in thought. Rhys loved the way she kept biting her lip. She always did it when she was nervous. Part of the reason why he loved her so much was how mercurial and mysterious she was, but now, he wished he could just read her mind.

'I'm glad you don't hate me,' Kelsey finally said, so quietly Rhys could hardly hear her. He shivered suddenly. The air was colder, and the sun had dipped below the trees behind him. He couldn't imagine a cold, dark, New York City winter without Kelsey by his side. Now was the time, and he needed to just grow a pair and do it already.

'I'd never hate you. You have to know that. In fact, I've been miserable without you, and I wish I hadn't given you up so easily. If there's somebody else, fine, but you need to know that I want to be your boyfriend still. I'll be the best boyfriend ever, if you'll just give me another chance,' he said in a rush. His heart was thumping wildly in his chest, like he'd just done two laps of butterfly, and he bit his lip nervously, watching Kelsey's face intently. What if she told him to stop being such a lame, pathetic loser? *Grow a sack, Sterling,* he thought to himself.

'I was really, really hoping that's why you'd asked me here.' Kelsey finally nodded, her blue eyes seemingly shadowed by sadness. Rhys wished he could wrap his arms around her and tell her it'd be okay, but he couldn't. Not yet. 'There is no one else . . . I mean, you're amazing, and I . . . Yes. I'd love to date again,' she said, her voice breaking on the last word. Rhys squeezed his eyes closed to make sure it wasn't a dream, but it wasn't – it was true. She wanted him. 'I'm sorry,' she said. 'For everything.'

'I . . .' Rhys began, but he stopped. What more was there to say? That he hadn't been able to sleep because of her? That she was the reason he had this Wolverine meets–William Shakespeare beard? But, just then, he felt her fluttery, thin fingers on his hands. She placed her soft lips on his.

'I missed this,' she whispered.

Rhys pulled her close into him, smelling her apple-scented shampoo and feeling her tiny, delicate curves between his arms. She kissed him back hungrily. Her skin felt hot under his fingertips, even though it was getting colder outside. He pulled her closer to him, never, ever wanting to let go. This was *it*. He was almost glad they'd broken up. Maybe it was for the best. Maybe they'd needed that separation to get this close?

Maybe.

'Get a room!' a mom yelled at them as she walked past, pushing a Bugaboo stroller.

Oops. Rhys pulled away and watched Kat pop a jelly baby candy in her mouth. She looked so happy. He was too. Soon enough they'd need that room after all.

Not to mention a razor, stat!

looking for labels, looking for love

Baby sat on the concrete steps of Union Square on Tuesday after school, her face turned up to the sun. Surrounding her were the members of Underground Response, all dressed in Stella McCartney dresses, 3.1 by Phillip Lim skinny pants, and Rag & Bone waistcoats. They would have been the picture of Upper East Side sophistication, except for the fact that the guys were the ones dressed in the frilly frocks, and the girls were all decked out in slouchy hoodies and khakis.

Fashion police! We have a major emergency!

Baby smiled in satisfaction, pleased that so many people had turned up. She and Sydney had come up with the idea of shooting a back-to-school fashion spread for *Rancor*. A fashion issue, *especially* with well-known designers, would cause the bitchy girls of Constance to wet their pants in excited anticipation, then freak out when they saw the guys in girls' clothing. They had discussed it over red wine and, when they'd begun using phrases like *female-centered sexuality* and *rejecting binaries*, realized they might actually accomplish something beyond making *Rancor* a little less lame. Luckily, Webber had been only too happy to help, volunteering Underground Responders to the cause.

Constance girls would have no idea how to understand this type of mind-fuck.

The mostly-Columbia-undergrad group milled about the stone steps, happily chatting as if they were at a really weird party. Baby sighed with contentment as she watched the double takes of passersby. This was *so* much better than mingling with traditional couture-wearing attendees at the fancy parties Avery obsessed over.

Sydney stood next to the nearby Gandhi statue, frowning into a digital camera. Even from Baby's perch, she could tell Sydney had no clue what she was doing. Baby knew she should go over and help her, but right now, she was content just to sit back and observe. These people, like Mateo, really *got* it: that life was supposed to be fun. It kind of reminded her of the best parts of a Bertolucci film, where characters realized their essential selves.

'Hey!' Mateo's strong arms circled her from behind. She could smell his smoky breath.

'Hey!' Baby giggled nervously and gently pulled his hands off her. J.P. had said he might stop by later, and even though she and Mateo were just friends, she didn't want J.P. to see them touching.

'I have to go help Webber and Sydney.' She brushed off the back of her enormous tan Paul Smith cords. They were the smallest size possible, but were still way too large on Baby's skinny frame. She ambled over to the Gandhi statue, where Sydney was now animatedly arguing with Webber, his lanky body bedecked in a Thread sheath dress.

'Jesus, it's a fucking nightmare here.' Sydney sighed dramatically, even though she was grinning. 'Like, drag isn't enough, now all these guys want to strip outside

Forever 21 to protest consumerism. You can only do one thing at a time in a revolution, you know?' Sydney shrugged and turned her full attention to Webber. 'I don't *care* that they want to strip outside Forever 21. They *can* – I just need to get these shots first. Please?' She was wearing a pair of ridiculous-looking candy-cane seersucker shorts that Baby sincerely hoped no guy would ever buy, and a wifebeater, sans bra. Her nipple piercings were clearly visible, like little door-knockers.

Come in!

'It's not so much consumerism as capitalism, man. It's the trickle-down effect,' one of the URs explained in a voice Baby recognized, from years of dating Tom, as 100 percent stoner. He adjusted his ridiculous-looking fake boobs under a small white blouse that would have looked adorable on a girl but just looked obscene on a guy.

'They can do the protest in fifteen minutes!' Sydney conceded loudly. 'Remind me why I thought it was a good idea to freaking direct people who are self-proclaimed anarchists?' She sighed ruefully. 'Hey Baby, is that your boyfriend?'

Baby glanced over at Mateo, who was fake-wrestling his friend Fernando in their matching Catholic schoolgirl-style kilts. Around them, a small crowd had gathered.

'Your *official* boyfriend,' Sydney clarified. She rolled her eyes in the direction of University Place. J.P. was shuffling along, carrying his BlackBerry, a MacBook Air bulging from his leather Tumi bag. He looked out of place in the park, which was filled with skateboarders, overly pierced NYU kids, and middle-aged people wearing '60s-inspired shapeless ground-length skirts and tie-dyed T-shirts.

'Is he coming from a Young Republican convention or a debate team meeting?' Sydney giggled.

'He's not like that, really,' Baby whispered, grabbing Sydney's digital camera and pretending to be particularly interested in the shots. They actually looked *good*, Baby realized, especially the faraway ones, where you really couldn't tell who was a girl and who was a guy.

'Hey gorgeous!'

Baby quickly passed the camera over to Sydney and wheeled around, smiling sheepishly. She hadn't told J.P. exactly what they were doing this afternoon, and she was pretty sure he wouldn't get it.

'You look . . . different,' he said skeptically.

At least he didn't say *pretty* this time.

'Yeah, we're sort of doing this fashion shoot thing that explores gender perceptions,' Baby explained. J.P. nodded, but he seemed unconvinced. Did it sound *dumb*? It hadn't when she'd talked it through with Sydney. Sydney bent down and picked up a bullhorn. 'Okay, people, let's get the shot!' she bleated like a Girl Scout leader. Around them, hordes of skirt-wearing guys formed a crowd on the steps.

'Why are you doing this again?' J.P. glanced around, backing away from the group.

Baby chewed her lip thoughtfully. J.P. looked nothing like Mateo or Webber or any of the other guys, and not just because he was the only guy not wearing a skirt. 'It's just fun.' Baby gazed into J.P.'s warm brown eyes imploringly.

'It's kind of getting cold,' J.P. responded noncommittally, as if they were strangers. Baby shivered involuntarily.

'Would it be better if I got you a skirt? My treat!' she teased, but she felt a little nervous. Everything was fine before J.P. had arrived but now all she could think about was what he'd think of all this.

'That's okay,' J.P. said stiffly. 'You know what, I should just go. I know you have to do this for school, so just call me when you're done. Maybe we can grab dinner or something.' He shrugged.

'Sorry,' Baby said, then felt angry at herself for apologizing. It wasn't *her* fault J.P. was uncomfortable. She personally was having a ball. 'Is it because you don't like women to wear the pants?' she joked lamely, gesturing to her cords.

J.P. chuckled, but his eyes darted away. 'Call me when you're done, doll,' he said, and practically sprinted out of the park. Baby walked back to the group. Doll? Since when was she anyone's doll?

Maybe since she started playing dress-up?

o does it his way

The Ninety-second Street Y's locker room was the usual mayhem of weekend excitement on Friday after practice. Owen walked through the cloud of Axe body spray emanating from the JV team's row of lockers. He roughly opened his own locker, ignoring the makeshift bar Hugh had set up in his swim bag, complete with sterling silver martini shakers from Tiffany.

'Need a gaytini, man?' Hugh called out cheerfully.

'No thanks, I'm cool.' Owen rolled his eyes and pulled his maroon St Jude's sweatshirt over his head. He was so over the gay thing, but he didn't really want to advertise his imaginary relationship. He hadn't heard from Jack in a few days, and it wasn't like he was going to call her or anything, so he didn't know if the whole thing was even going to happen.

'Hey, what's up?' Rhys asked as he edged by Owen to get to his locker. This practice had been his best ever. He'd nailed all his times, clocking Owen in *every* stroke, and even shaved half a second off his hundred-yard-backstroke time. Everything was *so* much better, or would be, once he and Kelsey had time alone to fully . . . consummate their relationship. He'd been thinking about it so much that even the word *organic* sounded dirty when their ancient teacher, Mr Kliesh, kept repeating it in AP chem. He'd tried to grab Owen to tell him about Kelsey, but he hadn't had a chance to talk one-on-one. It was like Owen was avoiding him. Maybe he just felt weird about the gay thing. *Was* he gay? He *was* awfully well groomed.

Says the guy who gets monthly facials.

'Hey, I have a quick announcement, guys,' Rhys yelled authoritatively, pleased at the way his deep voice echoed off the metal lockers. He certainly *sounded* in charge. From the depths of the locker room, he heard Hugh and Eli's groans. They probably thought he was going to give the halfhearted 'no drinking in season' speech he still hadn't gotten around to giving.

Not quite.

'So, guys, you know that the auction is next week,' Rhys began seriously. He climbed onto the wobbly wooden bench, hoping he wouldn't fall off.

'And . . .' Rhys trailed off, looking at the motley crew of guys surrounding him. Two-hundred-pound Ken looked like he had just come out from a year living in a cabin in the woods. Scrawny Chadwick had several random tufts of hair on his face, as if he had glued them on in the dark after doing Jaegerbombs. Because of their ridiculous chastity pact, they were all heinous looking. But not for long.

'And, for the occasion . . . you guys are gonna have to shave!'

Hugh Moore began clapping as he walked over to Rhys and offered up a bottle of Tanqueray. 'Way to go, Sterling! I knew you and Kelsey were going to seal the deal. That picnic setup? Brilliant!'

'Well . . .' Rhys turned red. They still hadn't done *it*. But they would. 'We're back together, and it's all going to happen,' he finished. 'Soon,' he added confidently, stepping off the bench.

'Oh my God, thank Jesus!' Hugh kneeled on the ground and kissed Rhys's feet.

'Okay, guys, let's do an emergency trip to Barneys' lingerie department. That's where the ladies are. Who's with me?' Hugh rolled his blue eyes crazily as he stroked his blondish beard. Rhys smiled and high-fived Hugh.

'So, uh, any guys you're crushing on?' Eli Smith asked Owen awkwardly as the rest of the team stepped up to congratulate Rhys.

But Owen didn't hear. He felt like he'd been run over by a truck. It was official: Rhys and Kelsey were back together.

'Actually, I'm bringing my new girlfriend, Jack Laurent. You know, that hot ballerina from Constance?' Owen said, the words tumbling out of his mouth before he could stop them.

'Wait, so you're a *ballerina*?' Hugh asked, turning away from Rhys.

'No!' Owen briefly lost patience. 'Jack – my new girl-friend – is a ballerina.' Suddenly, Coach popped his head in from the adjacent windowless office. Hugh hurriedly stuck the Tanqueray bottle in the lap pocket of Chadwick's sweatshirt and smiled angelically.

Nice save.

'Carlyle, doing good, you minx!' Coach grinned. 'I *love* the idea of playing the gay card to get the ladies. In fact, mind if I borrow it from you?' he asked hopefully.

Owen shrugged. Too much was happening right now,

and his brain felt fuzzy, as if he had spent way too much time underwater without coming up for air.

'You were our golden ticket for the auction, but now that you're paired off . . .' Coach assessed the motley gang of swimmers. 'Hugh, you're my Bachelor Number One. Don't disappoint me, bro,' he said, stalking back into his office.

'That's great, man!' Rhys pulled on a hoodie and glanced at Owen. 'Why'd you keep it a secret?'

'I don't know.' Owen stuffed his goggles in his maroon swim bag and slung it over his shoulder. 'It all just happened.'

'So let's do something soon! I know Jack a little, but I haven't seen her since, like, eighth-grade ballroom dance classes.'

'Ballroom? And they think *I'm* gay?' Owen meant it to be a joke, but it came out sounding like a bark.

'Everyone did it.' Rhys shrugged defensively as they walked out the doors of the Y. He pulled out his Treo and quickly texted a message to Kelsey.

Owen's heart pounded against his chest, the way it did after an all-out sprint. Even knowing Rhys was texting Kelsey made him feel like his world was totally fucking falling apart.

'I'm just asking Kelsey if dinner sometime next week would be cool. Maybe Tuesday? I kind of want to hang out, just the two of us, this weekend,' Rhys explained. He smiled at his friend, feeling giddy at the prospect of a double date. The two girls could chitchat, Rhys and Owen could hang out, and everyone would love it!

All they need is a picket fence and matching Jaguars.

'Okay,' Owen said glumly. His stomach was churning.

What did Rhys mean he wanted to be *alone* with Kelsey this weekend? And a double date? While he desperately wanted to see Kelsey, he knew he needed to stay as far away from her as possible. If she hated him now, she'd hate him even *more* if she thought he'd found a girlfriend so quickly. Owen sighed sadly. Jack seemed like a nice girl, and was so cute with her reddish hair that perfectly matched her freckles. But she just wasn't *Kelsey*.

'Owen!' He heard a lilting girl's voice and whirled around. There, standing on the corner in a simple black knee-length dress and suede heels, was Jack. It was as if he'd conjured her.

'Oh . . . hey!' he called, trying to sound enthusiastic as he walked down the steps of the Y toward her. He was completely aware that all the guys were watching him.

'I wanted to know what our plans are for tonight. I also love seeing you after you work out!' Jack said chirpily, not missing a beat. For pretending to be a girlfriend, she actually sounded surprisingly . . . *girlfriendy*.

Imagine that.

Owen racked his brain. He remembered his mom planning a dinner party, but as far as he knew, neither of his sisters was bringing any friends. It was easier to fend for themselves when it came to dinner parties with Edie's group of hippie artist friends. The ones she'd invited tonight had all performed together in an experimental production of *Waiting for Godot* in the '70s, where they'd all appeared nude, painted blue. Thankfully, Owen had never seen any pictures. He hoped they weren't planning on doing a re-creation tonight.

That's one way of breaking the ice.

'Um, well, my mom's throwing this dinner thing at my

house . . .' He trailed off, aware that all the guys were eyeing him curiously. He draped his arm around Jack protectively and walked away from the prying eyes of his teammates. He was surprised at how toned her arm felt. She smelled like a mixture of lavender, sugar, and Tiger Balm, the anti-inflammatory ointment he used on sore muscles.

'Great, I guess we should get going then. I'd love to buy some flowers for your mom and maybe your sisters too,' Jack said sweetly as she allowed Owen to lead her across the crosswalk. She cuddled into him, wishing that J.P. could see her now. She was surprised at how solid Owen felt. He had the same really taut arm muscles the male dancers she worked with did. She always trusted them to lift her up and never, ever let go. When she had been with J.P., she always sort of felt like he would drop her. Which, thinking about it, he sort of had.

She smiled at him flirtily, aware that all his teammates were watching them. It was kind of fun. She loved being the center of attention. And as a partner, she really could do worse than Owen Carlyle.

Has the queen of the Upper East Side found a new king?

where are a's party people at?

Avery barged into the penthouse on Friday evening after a solo trip to Barneys. She had gone to make herself feel better, but browsing through the racks alone, without friends to tell her what was too last-season and what pants made her butt look flat, just made her feel lonelier than ever. Even though she knew her mom's dinner party was a totally lame way to spend a Friday night, she was actually glad to have something to do.

She was momentarily taken aback when she saw a large blue Balenciaga bag slung on the low couch in the living room. That bag wasn't Baby's, and it *definitely* wasn't her mother's. Edie preferred to tote her belongings in a hemp sack batiked with pink elephants.

Avery felt a wave of annoyance. It was probably one of Owen's conquests, or maybe one of Baby's new weirdo friends. While her siblings were having fun in New York City, she was on the freaking *leash* of the board of overseers. They had 'meetings' practically every afternoon. They were supposed to begin planning a mid-fall auction for Constance, or at least that's what Muffy had said yesterday when Avery had been called out of calculus to speak to her. Instead, they'd met at the stuffy, old-lady-smelling

National Arts Club. She'd spent four hours listening to the board compare notes on which luxury cruise lines had the highest ratio of available widowed men to unattached women.

Maybe she should tag along with them over spring break.

'Hello?' Avery called. She heard voices coming from the living room and hurriedly stamped across the entranceway, pausing to throw her coat in her bedroom. She wished Edie's circle of artist friends could include some scruffy, cute artists, like the ones who hung out at Beatrice Inn or the Waverly. Edie still clung to the idea that her friends were undiscovered geniuses, not realizing that a lack of talent was a big part of why they'd spent the last two decades toiling in obscurity in godforsaken places like Brooklyn. At least Edie had gotten out in time to have a life, Avery realized as she stalked across the apartment and smoothed her hair behind her ears.

'Ave? You home?' Owen called from the kitchen, followed by a girly giggle. Avery walked into the kitchen and stopped in her tracks. Perched at the marble center island, daintily sipping a glass of champagne, was none other than bitch-supreme Jack Laurent, clad in a high-necked Tocca dress. Avery had been purposefully avoiding her ever since her cruel revelation in the cafeteria, but to see her now, up close and in *her* apartment – with her *brother* – was just too much.

'Avery, hello darling.' Jack hopped off her stool and walked over to kiss Avery on both cheeks.

Fancy meeting you here!

Avery narrowed her eyes and held on to the counter for balance. Owen seemed amused by the whole thing. He leaned back and sipped his champagne, looking totally relaxed. Through the French doors, Avery could hear laughter mixed with what sounded like a bagpipe.

'Hey Ave,' Owen greeted cheerily as he waved a Brie-slathered cracker in her general direction. 'Did Jack tell you we were hanging out?'

'No,' Avery said brusquely. She hadn't told Owen that much about Jack, but still, couldn't he have just felt her bitch vibes radiating? Jack subtly put her hand near Owen's and Avery's stomach churned angrily. After all, they'd spent nine months in the womb together! This was like a bad horror movie.

Invasion of the brother-snatchers!

'Anyway, want a glass?' Not waiting for an answer, Owen pulled a tumbler out of one of the smooth oak cabinets and liberally splashed Veuve inside as if it were water. 'You'll need this much,' Owen said knowingly as Avery grabbed the glass.

Oh, he has no idea.

'Cheers.' Owen held up his own glass. 'We're hiding out for a little bit. They're starting performances soon.' He picked up a turdlike object from a paper bag and waggled it at Avery. 'Carob bar?'

'No thanks.' Avery smiled tightly.

'Hello?' Baby banged into the kitchen, wearing an ugly blue polo shirt that said BEST BUY on it. She'd belted it and was wearing it as a dress over a pair of Wolford black fishnet stockings that Avery suddenly recognized as ones *she* had bought. What the fucking fuck? Could her life get any more ridiculous?

Does she even need to ask?

'What's *she* doing here?' Baby narrowed her eyes at Jack

and put her hands on her tiny hips. The T-shirt gave her an air of authority, like she was a store manager or something. Avery hoped she was just wearing it to be ironic, or as part of something she had to do for that dumb improv group. She hoped Baby hadn't actually gotten a *job*. Just then, Edie walked in with several of her artsy friends, including one large, redheaded guy wearing a kilt and a buttoned-up white dress shirt with ruffles.

'We're making a stew!' Edie crowed. 'It's an African tribal recipe that's supposed to be good luck for when a family moves to a new hut. I thought it was fitting for breaking in our kitchen. We can all help, like one big family.' Edie's eyes shone as she opened the cabinets and haphazardly pulled out utensils.

Avery winced. Why couldn't she just live in a nice, normal house where a family dinner meant a simple filet mignon served by the maid in a formal front room? She could *not* deal with this right now. She stalked into the cavernous living room, set up with elaborate pillows and tablecloths on the floor.

'Can we *please* sit in chairs? Maybe even at the dining room table?' Avery hissed to her mother as she flitted manically between the kitchen and the dining room. At this point, she'd rather turn around and go straight to the King Cole Bar, where Muffy and Esther had gleefully planned to spend the evening drinking scotch and sodas.

Hmm, maybe she should invite them over for some tribal stew!

'Nonsense, this is so much more fun! Who wants a stuffy dinner party?' Edie's eyes twinkled merrily and she smoothed the wrinkles in her floor-length black dress. She looked like a gray-blond vampire.

'Thank you *so* much for having me here, Mrs Carlyle,' Jack gushed, trailing in behind them. 'Just let me know what I can do. This is all so wonderfully *unique*!' She smirked at Avery, but Edie didn't notice the sarcasm.

'Thank you, darling.' Edie looked around. 'I don't need anything now – just start thinking about your performance piece.' She rested her bony hand on Jack's forearm and gave her a maternal smile. Jack smiled back uncertainly. Performance piece? What the fuck?

'My mom likes to have everyone perform something at her dinner parties. It's sort of a Carlyle tradition, but don't worry, we can totally leave before then,' Owen explained, coming to her rescue. Jack grinned. She couldn't believe Avery Carlyle, of the preppy Marc Jacobs headbands and the pink Filofax, had such a fruitcake for a mom. She couldn't wait to see what *else* Avery was hiding.

'What an *interesting* sculpture collection.' Jack wandered over to an elaborate antique Chippendale cabinet set up in the corner of the room, where Edie had placed a collection of small glass octopi she had found at a Brooklyn flea market.

'You think so!' Edie clapped her hands. 'I'm glad *you* like them. Avery of course doesn't appreciate them. She doesn't understand that today's kitsch is art.' She shook her head sadly. Her artist friends had gathered around a large orange Le Creuset pot.

'I brought my sousaphone,' a skinny guy announced to the general group.

Shut the fuck up! Avery wanted to scream. She knocked back a glass of champagne, standing next to Jack as if they were best friends or something. Jack was acting like she was so fucking interested in everything, when for all Avery knew she was filming the whole ridiculous chain of events and live-feeding it to everyone at Constance. She inhaled deeply, determined *not* to give Jack the pleasure of a breakdown.

'Jack's a dancer. Maybe she and you could do something together, Owen,' Avery suggested sweetly.

'Great!' Edie clapped her hands together. 'You both can provide pre-dinner entertainment!' Edie frowned into the pot. 'I think this might be done.'

'Looks terrific,' Avery said, scanning the room of ten or so artists, annoyed that Baby had disappeared. Together they needed to hold some type of intervention to let Owen know who – or better yet, *what* – his new girlfriend was.

Baby slunk back into the living room, finally rescuing Avery from her personal circle of hell. She had changed into a simple black dress and her hair was loose around her shoulders. She winked at Avery and sat down next to Jack, elbowing her as if they were best friends sharing a delicious secret.

Psst, I stole your ex-boyfriend! Tee-hee!

'This is so nice. You know, I was just talking with my boyfriend, J.P., about how we might like to travel to Africa this summer,' Avery heard Baby say to Jack. She smiled to herself. Sometimes Baby really could come through. Still, she wasn't sure how much longer she could deal with Jack in her fucking living room.

'Hey Owen, I need to talk to you. You too, Baby,' Avery pulled them both to a stand. She had had enough. It was one thing for Jack Laurent to edge her out of Constance, but this was Avery's territory, and she was never a girl to go down without a fight. She dragged Owen onto the terrace, her manicured fingernails poking half-moon circles into his smooth, hairless forearm.

'Ow, Ave, what's your problem?'

The three siblings stepped onto the terrace. The night air was cool, and the windows in the surrounding apartments were lit up, tiny yellow boxes against the dark night sky. Inside those apartments were normal families and catered parties and actual, eligible boys, Avery thought as she looked across the street wistfully.

'Why are you with Jack Laurent?' She turned back to Owen, her eyes narrowed.

Owen paused. Avery had always gotten into his business, but she'd never been this mad about anything before. He looked over to Baby for help, but her dark eyes were narrowed at him as well. Why did his sisters care so much?

'We're dating.' Owen shrugged defensively. He was so sick of everyone questioning his personal life.

Aw, can't we all just get along?

'You're dating the girl who sent me to *jail*!' Avery said indignantly, sloshing her wine on the concrete slab of the terrace.

Owen laughed. '*She* put you in jail?'

'Well, she called the cops at my party, which is pretty much the same thing,' Avery huffed. 'Fine, date her. Date the Antichrist. I don't care.' Avery stomped off, almost stepping on Rothko.

Owen thought about it. Jack might not be as sweet as she appeared, and she might have ulterior motives. But no one was that evil. Besides, it would be nice to get to know a girl in New York. His sisters were totally overreacting. Maybe Avery had totally misunderstood Jack.

And maybe someone's already forgotten about another girl's apple-scented shampoo?

Owen walked back inside, pausing when he saw the way Jack's hair fell over her slim shoulders. The candlelight captured her hair, making it look like it was on fire. She seemed so alive and fun. Meanwhile, Avery and Baby were huddled against each other, scowling. They were probably just jealous. Owen shrugged it off.

'Hey kids!' Edie said, pulling herself off the floor. 'I just got your invitations for the St Jude's swim team benefit,' she announced. She pulled out three already opened envelopes and Avery made a mental note to open her own private PO box. The invitations were elegantly engraved with the maroon St Jude's crest. 'It says you each can bring a date. So, who are you bringing?' Edie plopped down on a pillow between the four of them, hardly registering that Jack wasn't one of her children.

'I'm going with J.P. We're really excited about it,' Baby said, smiling innocently at Jack.

Jack sniffed, trying to ignore the jab. She smiled angelically at the Carlyles' weirdo mom. Although, in the long run, she'd probably enjoy having this wackjob of a mom more than her own.

'Well, obviously, you and Owen are going together, so the important question is, who is Avery going to bring?' Edie mused. 'Do you know she's never had a boyfriend?' Edie addressed Jack like she was spouting harmless trivia. 'Not even in kindergarten, and you know how horny five-year-olds are! All the inhibitions come in later.' Edie shook her head.

'How sad,' Jack murmured, fluttering her heavily mascaraed eyelashes at Avery. Avery recognized that look. It was the final glance a lioness gave before she ate her prey. Avery had two words running through her head: *oh* and *shit*. Jack was poor and lived in an attic with her crazy, mentally unstable mom, but it didn't even matter. By tomorrow, the entire world would know Avery was a complete freak of nature. She felt a dull ache in her chest.

'Okay, well, we're doing performances in the next room. I'd love to see some interpretive dancing. I remember Avery and Baby did a great one a few years ago.'

Jack smiled but didn't even ask Edie to hear more about it. She didn't need to. Even an embarrassing story about Avery and Baby performing a vernal equinox step dance in lace-up sandals was nothing compared to the information Jack already had in her possession.

'I think I have to go,' Jack demurred, smoothing her dress and picking up her bag. 'Owen, I can't wait until the benefit. And it'll be great to see you there too, Baby,' she added, making it sound more like an insult than anything.

'Okay, I guess I'll just walk Jack out,' Owen said uncertainly, looking from one sister to another. From Avery's blue, flashing eyes to Baby's brown, narrowed ones, he felt like he was asking them permission.

As Owen and Jack made their way out the door, Avery could hear them laughing into the hallway, the sound mixing with the farting noises of bagpipes in the background. What a swell night.

Just wait till the morning!

partners in crime

Owen whisked Jack past the doorman and into the chilly September night. He briefly put his arm around her shoulders, then retracted it as if he'd touched something right out of the microwave. Was he allowed to do that?

Is there a *Rules: Fake Boyfriend* edition?

'Thanks for dinner,' Jack said. Now that they weren't performing in front of anyone, it suddenly felt awkward talking to him. She glanced at Owen's dumb NANTUCKET PIRATES T-shirt. He looked like such a *boy*, especially compared to J.P., who always looked like he was late for a power lunch at Capital Grille.

'Why'd you call the cops on my sister's party?' he asked suddenly.

'It's a long story.' Jack shrugged, hoping she'd sound mysterious instead of bitchy.

'Avery's pretty mad at you.'

'I'll apologize to her. It was just something silly. Like a welcome to New York initiation. You know.' Jack shrugged again. 'So, tell me about Kelsey.' She changed the subject.

Owen sighed in frustration. So he had accidentally gotten involved with a girl who was involved with Rhys. But he hadn't even known that at the time. Did that mean he had to walk around with a scarlet *A* on his chest? He'd thought New York would be a chance to start over, but clearly he was in over his head. And Owen hated nothing more than feeling like he was drowning. 'Nothing is going on between us. Why, what are you going to tell people?' he spat out angrily.

'You want the truth?' Jack asked. 'I'm not going to say anything,' she said honestly, surprising herself. 'Can we please go to the St Jude's benefit together? We both need dates,' she rationalized. *Good.* That made her sound a little bit less desperate.

'So then why did you . . .' Owen trailed off and awkwardly crossed his arms over his thin gray T-shirt. He *really* didn't understand girls. Still, something about Jack seemed so sweet and innocent.

Looks can be deceiving.

'My mom is French. And crazy and moving back to Paris for some senior citizen reality television show. My dad has all these kids with his wife, who's, like, a teenager practically. My boyfriend broke up with me for your sister, and I just could use some support,' Jack said in a rush of words.

So much for subtlety.

'Okay.' Owen nodded. 'Family can get complicated. Besides, I sort of like doing the fake-dating dating thing,' he added, because it was true.

Jack nodded. It was sort of nice to talk to Owen. Even if his sisters had pretty much ruined her life.

'Um, do you need me to walk you home?' Owen asked, shifting uncomfortably on the pavement. He really didn't want to go back into the claustrophobic apartment, and now that everything with Jack was out in the open, he felt curiously relaxed. Maybe he could ask her opinion on what he should do to get over Kelsey. He needed a friend.

What happened to that swim team buddy of his?

'No, I'm fine.' She pulled out her Treo and frowned. 'Everyone's heading to the Beatrice Inn tonight.' Jack shrugged and turned her face up to Owen's. 'You want to come?' She'd asked just to be polite, but found herself hoping he'd say yes.

Owen paused. Too many thoughts were jumbled together in his head and he wasn't sure what to do. If he went with Jack, would it be for real, or would it just be another public appearance? 'Well . . .' he began, then trailed off as he took in her catlike green eyes, her freckles against her pale skin, the curve of her hipbones through her dress, even though she was muscular and athletic. The muscles on her arms reminded him of the way waves looked right before they crested on a clear Nantucket day.

Owen's hesitation made Jack suddenly panic. 'I've got to jet. See you later!' she said quickly, turning on her fragile stilettos and practically running down Fifth Avenue.

Owen watched her retreating back in confusion. What was that about? He shook his head and turned, entering the building.

'Women,' the hat-wearing, grandfatherly doorman said as he pulled open the imposing black doors. He guffawed, slapping his knee loudly as if he'd heard a really good joke. Owen stiffened. Had the doorman been listening? It felt like *everyone* was always watching in New York.

That's because we are.

Owen quickly strode to the elevator bank, aware of how

his steps echoed on the ultra-polished marble floor of the lobby. He really hoped Edie's guests had gone home and weren't using the penthouse as a crash pad or an interpretive dance space or something equally bizarre. He needed time to think.

About what? Or whom?

He opened the unlocked penthouse door. Immediately, he was accosted by Avery and Baby.

'We're not finished here. Are you seriously going to keep dating Jack?' Baby demanded, her hands on her tiny hips. Avery stood next to her. Owen was reminded of a pair of mismatched bookends they used to have at their house in Nantucket.

'Yes,' he countered easily, but there was a slight edge to his voice.

'Owen, she's not right for you,' Avery said, trying to sound like the voice of reason. In Nantucket, she'd worked for a peer-counseling hotline, where kids called in with all sorts of emotional traumas. The school psychologist had recommended statements like *I understand* or *I hear.* Avery took a deep breath and readjusted her headband. 'I understand you think Jack Laurent is hot,' Avery began, eyeing Owen, who was shuffling uncomfortably from one Adidas slide to the other. 'But looks only go so far,' she said delicately, wishing she could say what she was really thinking – that Jack was a bitch in ballerina's clothing.

'It's more than that. She's funny and honest and a hard worker and an athlete,' Owen explained, just wanting his sisters to bug off already. He had no desire to explain that Jack was blackmailing him, or why. But even as he delivered a laundry list of Jack's accomplishments, he realized what he'd said was mostly true.

'What, a couple pirouettes in a pink tutu and she's an *athlete*?' Baby said sharply.

'You know, I don't know what you girls are doing at Constance, but maybe you can try to all be friends,' Owen snapped, annoyed. 'I don't have time for this.' With that, he stomped off to his room.

As Owen huffed off, Baby felt a little guilty for yelling at him. After all, he'd never said anything bad about her pot-smoking loser Nantucket boyfriend – although, thinking about it, she sort of wished he had. She looked over at Avery, who was hugging Rothko to her body so hard his yellow eyes were bulging out. 'Are you okay?'

'I'm fine.' Avery let go of Rothko, who hissed and scampered away. She stomped behind him, making a beeline for her bedroom, and threw herself down on her white eyelet bedspread, looking up at the ceiling's delicate molding. Her life was falling apart and no one seemed to care. She had no boyfriend. No friends. Even the cat didn't want to hang out with her.

She held her hand up over her face and glanced at her silver Rolex. It was only ten o'clock on a Friday night. She wondered where Genevieve, Jiffy, and Sarah Jane were. She wondered if her life would *ever* be the way she had imagined it would be: full of dinner parties, after-school functions, and out-of-control nights.

'Hey Babe?' she called. She suddenly felt completely lonely.

'Are you okay?' her tiny sister asked in concern, opening the door. She climbed onto the bed and bounced up and down on her knees, the way she used to when they were little.

'I guess so.' Avery paused dramatically, waiting for Baby

to say something that would make everything okay. Baby knew better than anyone that greasy food, vodka, and a dumb '80s teen movie could always make Avery feel better.

Just then, Baby's cell beeped.

'Is that Mr New York?' Avery asked, surprised by how bitter she sounded. After all, it wasn't Baby's fault that the most successful and cutest high school boy in Manhattan had fallen in love with Baby instead of her.

Tell us how you really feel.

'Probably. I guess his Save the Indigenous Salamanders or whatever benefit ended early.' Baby pulled her cell from her pocket. Her face flushed and she quickly snapped the phone shut again.

'I want to see!' Avery squealed. She reached into Baby's pocket, pulled out the slim red Nokia, and flipped it open.

Party in Bushwick tonight. Want to come? Bring your 'kick the patriarchy' friend. No one else. Avery looked up at Baby questioningly. Did Baby have a secret boyfriend?

And can she borrow him? Two fake boyfriends are even better than one!

'It's just this guy from that improv thing. I think he wants me and Sydney to film something for *Rancor*. You want to come?' Baby shrugged, looking so sweet and innocent that Avery briefly felt bad for thinking she might be having an illicit love affair. Avery considered. She might be boyfriendless, but she certainly wasn't going to hang out with unshaven, overpierced, pretentious hipsters in *Brooklyn* of all places.

'Not really,' Avery said regally, and flopped back onto the pillows. But sat up sharply as she realized Baby was rummaging through her closet. 'If you take *anything* with a tag still on it, I'll kill you,' Avery threatened, even though at this point, she'd rather kill herself.

Or maybe she should start a blog – misery loves company.

gossipgirl.net *Disclaimer: All the real names of places, people, and events have been altered or abbreviated to protect the innocent. Namely, me.*

topics   sightings   your e-mail   post a question

hey people!

Joan of Arc. Queen Elizabeth 1. Edie Bouvier Beale. Katharine Hepburn. That's just a small sampling of names from the long history of eccentric single women. Now we can add one more to their ranks: it seems the lustrous and elegant **A** is also manless – and always has been. Does that mean she has a future wearing unusual outfits, surrounded by cats and fabulous gay men? Only time will tell. But before you judge, think about it. There are *advantages* to not having a man around:

You can eat a whole box of Godiva in bed and not worry about chocolate stains, pimples, or cellulite. Who's looking?

You can adopt the entire population of cats at Bideawee animal shelter *and* spend all your money buying them mini coats from Marc Jacobs. The best part? They can't say no!

You can wear a freaky mink stole with the animal head still attached, and no one will try to stop you.

Basically, when you stop trying to impress the opposite sex, you can do whatever the hell you want. And maybe, fifty years down the road, there'll be a *Harper's Bazaar* fashion spread dedicated to your unusual sense of style. Or you could die miserable and alone in a cat pee–soaked apartment. Either one!

charity begins at home

As a certain school fund-raiser approaches, I've been thinking about the spirit of giving. Everybody thinks charity is just about sparing some change, but why not access your inner Good Samaritan and try simply being *nice*? Start with your nearest and dearest, and the sentiment is sure to spread outward. Meet Daddy for lunch at the Harvard Club and try to listen as he drones on about his new schooner. Let your mom buy you that dorky hooded Norma Kamali coat – the one she loves, but which makes you look like an extra from *Harry Potter*. Take a moment to bond with your brothers or sisters, even if they *are* totally annoying. After all, doesn't love make the world go round? And speaking of . . .

couple corner

It's come to my attention that some people need to get their gaydar checked. The luscious but masculine **O** *does* have an eye for the ladies – specifically, one freckle-faced ballerina who's been having a tough time lately. Is her luck changing? And was *she* the girl our favorite flipper boy was holding out for? If so, then good for them both. They're almost too pretty to be true.

sightings

A at **Goodman's Café** on the seventh floor of **Bergdorf's**, showing off her purchases to a group of blue-haired, St John–clad old ladies. And she wonders why she doesn't have a BF? Or a BFF? **J** taking extra ballet classes at **Steps** . . . **O** doing extra laps at the Ninety-second Street Y. Why don't they burn calories together? **B** and **J.P.** in Central Park, frolicking with their iPods with that back-to-nature hippie group. Sounds like a great way to bond as a couple! Until, that is, **J.P.** made a secret phone call to his dad behind a tree. Didn't anyone tell him it's about being in the moment? The triplets' mom, **E**, carrying a bagpipe down Fifth. Everyone loves a parade!

your e-mail

Q: Dear Gossip Girl,

So, now that **J** and **O** are together, does that mean that **A** and **J** are back to being friends? Since **J**'s practically in the family and all?

– LoveandRainbows

A: Dear LandR,

Who needs friends when you've got frenemies?

– Gossip Girl

Q: Yo, G Squared,

Hey. Heard about this site from my little sister. I go to this boarding school in Massachusetts and my soccer buddy has these totally gnarly teeth because he said this girl from Nantucket totally, like, knocked them out. I think it's **A**. Apparently, she has, like, wicked anger management issues and she takes them out on the guys she crushes on, which is why she's never had a boyfriend. Just a warning to the fellas out there.

– Buddd

A: Dear B,

Warning taken. I guess we won't get on **A**'s bad side. Except for the few that are already there . . . Maybe they should invest in mouth guards.

– GG

Q: Dear Gossip Girl,

I really like this girl but trouble is I am from Spain and she is from New York. Do you think she would come back to my homeland with me?

– Happy Wanderer

A: Dear HW,

While the idea of spending September by the Spanish seaside sounds intriguing, you should ask yourself a question: is the girl you speak of a HW herself?

– GG

Q: Dear GG,

U are so totes the Carlyles' mom!

– Conspiracy Theory

A: Dear CT,

Um, no. Although I do admire her spirit!

– GG

Phew! With so much going on, I'm just going to focus on the *R*'s: reflexology at Mario Badescu, rosé at Beatrice, and Rodarte's fall line. Sometimes it's the simple pleasures that give life meaning.

You know you love me,

GOSSIP GIRL

boy story

Avery sat in the elegant drawing room of Esther Klepfisz's penthouse in the Sherry-Netherland hotel on Fifth Avenue and Fifty-ninth Street, trying not to fall asleep. The apartment was beautifully decorated by 1950s standards but looked like it hadn't been renovated or even deep cleaned since the Eisenhower administration. Avery wrinkled her nose at the dust mites that were all too apparent in the afternoon sunlight. Today, the discussion was whether or not it was appropriate to rename the computer lab after a wealthy donor who'd passed away during the summer and willed everything to Constance. Unfortunately, the deceased was named Emmaline Butz, which would render the computer lab 'the Butz Lab.'

Catchy.

Avery doodled her name on one of the blank pieces of pink paper at the back of her leather Filofax and sighed deeply, trying to tune out Esther's screechy argument that they should use Emmaline's *maiden* name. Whatever. At least Emmaline Butz had gotten married. Avery still couldn't believe that Jack Laurent had found out she'd never had a boyfriend. It was all people had been talking about at Constance, and she'd even gotten e-mails from lame little freshmen at schools all over the Upper East Side who felt sorry for her and wanted to offer advice. Even Sydney, the pierced-nipples girl everyone made fun of, had a boyfriend.

Avery looked down at the paper, now filled with her scripted name. She noted the elegant curve of her script; the way the *y* of her first name bled into the *C* of her last name. Was she destined to be Avery Carlyle forever?

Unless perhaps Mr Butz is looking for a new wife?

It didn't help that Muffy had begun calling her La Petite AC. The other ladies had taken it up as well, and when they addressed her, Avery felt like they were talking about a miniature air conditioner. Who wanted to date a small air conditioner?

'Tea is served,' a stringbeanlike maid announced in a scratchy voice as she burst through the French doors. She looked like she was about to tip over onto the Oriental carpet from the staggering weight of the silver tray.

'Put it on the side table,' Esther whined. Avery breathed a sigh of relief at the sudden flurry of activity as the board of overseers crowded around the tea tray. Even the ladies who'd fallen asleep during the meeting snapped to attention as soon as they heard the clink of silver against china.

Muffy, surprisingly agile for an eighty-year-old, tore to the front of the line. Once served, she slowly lowered herself down on the worn blue love seat next to Avery, her teacup rattling against its saucer, her knees creaking loudly.

'What's the matter, darling?' she crooned, stuffing a biscuit into her mouth. It crunched loudly, unleashing a spray of crumbs that mingled in the air with the dust mites. Avery shook her head miserably. Why couldn't she have just been born in 1932, when she would have had at least a chance at being cool?

'Is it boy trouble?' Muffy pressed her wrinkled hand against Avery's smooth, pink Essie Escapades-manicured one.

'No!' Avery cried. She *wished* she had boy trouble. She'd rather deal with a pot-smoking, forgetting-to-call boyfriend than no boyfriend at all.

I believe there's a newly single boy in Nantucket who fits that description perfectly.

'So what is it? You have the whole world at your disposal,' Muffy whispered enviously. 'Personally, I don't even know why you spend so much time with us.' She cocked her head toward Helen Lord, a Park Avenue doyenne who had recently divorced her oil tycoon husband. She was busily stuffing cookies in her snakeskin Bottega Veneta purse. 'She's been doing that for months,' Muffy huffed. 'We'd kick her off, but she's not doing any harm. We think she's just feeding her loneliness.'

Avery held back a sniffle. If Helen Lord was lonely, she and Avery had something in common. Maybe they could steal cookies and then run off together, like a really lame version of Thelma and Louise. Clearly that was the direction Avery was headed in, so why delay the inevitable?

'Sugar, you look like you're going to cry!' Muffy realized in concern as she ripped her gaze away from Helen. She held Avery's hand tightly. 'Are you sure there's nothing wrong?'

'I don't have a boyfriend,' Avery confessed. She looked down at her impeccable Constance Billard seersucker skirt, spread over her thin, tanned legs. At least she didn't look like a freaky old lady. *Yet.*

'So?' Muffy exclaimed, waving her teacup around and practically spilling Earl Grey on her light pink quilted Chanel purse. 'You shouldn't *need* a boyfriend. Pussycat, do you know how common boys are? You need to play the field!'

'But there's this fund-raiser I need a date for,' Avery said miserably as she bit her lip. Muffy's brown eyes were so wide and friendly and interested that she wanted to tell her everything. Next, she'd be spilling the story about how she'd knocked out the front tooth of the first boy she kissed.

Don't worry, the story's already been spilled.

'Oh, darling! You've just got to get out on the playing field. I mean, I married my first husband when I was eighteen. Poor thing couldn't get it up – he was an inexperienced mess!' Muffy laughed as Avery choked on her tea. *Get it up?* 'Luckily, my next husband had no problems in that department. His problem was in the ladies' lingerie department. He liked to wear it. Especially my pink brassieres.' Avery smiled politely. This was way too much information.

'Thanks for sharing,' she mumbled, turning bright red.

'Of course, dear. And don't worry about not having a boyfriend. Your time will come,' Muffy pronounced, loud enough for the entire room to hear. She stood up from the love seat.

The second Muffy moved away, a group of elderly ladies crowded around Avery, rooting in their Prada and Givenchy clutches. Avery's eyes widened. What was going on? Were they going to donate their spare change to some Help Boyfriendless Avery fund? Esther triumphantly fished something out of her pink Chanel wallet. It was . . . a photograph?

'A blond like you would go perfectly with my grandson Elliot!' Esther crowed, as if she were talking about a rare Louis XIV dining room set. She shoved a photograph in Avery's face, conveniently blocking Helen and the orange Hermès photo album she'd whipped out of her voluminous fuchsia crocodile Birkin bag. Avery plucked the photo from Esther's hands and examined it, expecting some dorky, zit-infested mathlete. Instead, she saw a picture of a guy standing on a pristine field, wearing a soccer uniform. He was tall, with shaggy blond hair, rugged features, and tanned arms and legs. Elliot was cute! Avery nodded eagerly as she felt Muffy's rigid fingernails digging into her arm.

'Don't listen to Esther,' Muffy whispered loudly, shooting a mutinous glance in her direction. 'We all know he's a divorce case waiting to happen. Just like his father,' she stage-whispered.

'Well, Muffy, we certainly all know about *your* impeccable taste in men,' Esther shot back, her voice dripping with sarcasm.

Muffy ignored her, a merry twinkle in her eye. 'Well, we're not talking about me, we're talking about La Petite AC. And for *her*, I'm only going to offer the best. My grandson Tristan!' Muffy crowed. Avery smiled, loving the attention. Muffy riffled through her purse and pulled out a photo of a guy standing on the front steps of a town house, his arms crossed over his chest. He seemed slightly self-conscious, like he was being forced to pose, but with his brown hair, sparkling deep-set blue eyes, and tanned skin, he looked like a Ralph Lauren model, just off a yacht docked in Newport. He was even more perfect than Elliot! This one was *just right*.

Calm down, Goldilocks.

'Tristan looks . . . *nice*,' Avery squeaked. She'd come dangerously close to saying *hot*. She beamed at the collection of geriatrics, still hopefully thrusting photographs at her. Just wait until she showed up at the swim team gala with a veritable posse of handsome escorts.

Hopefully *minus* their grandmas.

two's company, three's a crowd, and four is just trouble

Owen jogged easily across Madison on Tuesday afternoon, butterflies already forming in his stomach. Tonight was the night he and Jack were going out to dinner with Rhys and Kelsey. This would be the first time he'd see Kelsey since he'd so heartlessly told her she was just a one-night stand. When Rhys had called to give him the restaurant info, he'd almost faked sick, but he really couldn't delay the inevitable. Maybe it wouldn't be so bad seeing Kelsey with Rhys. Maybe somehow, the spell would be broken, and she'd just be another girl.

Or maybe not.

Owen quickened his pace. Even though they were meeting Rhys and Kelsey for dinner at 2Na – this new sushi fusion restaurant in Soho Rhys had been raving about – Jack had asked him to meet her at 3 Guys coffee shop. It was all the way up on Madison, totally out of the way.

And totally close to where a certain guy likes to walk his labradoodles?

The smell of fries and coffee assaulted Owen as he walked into the old-fashioned diner. He suddenly felt ridiculously hungry. Maybe they'd have time for him to order a pre-dinner? Tiny pieces of raw fish were definitely not part of a balanced diet. He spotted Jack, her back toward him, her shiny auburn hair pulled up into a high, glossy ponytail. He walked over, kind of nervous about interacting with her friends, especially the one with the crazy eyes and long bangs. She always tried to bump into him outside his apartment, or when he was in the middle of a swim team run around the reservoir.

Can't blame a girl for trying, right?

'Hey ladies,' Owen said as he sidled up to the table. Immediately, he wished he hadn't said that. It made him sound old and creepy. All he was missing was a Hugh Hefner–style smoking jacket and a cigar. Or, come to think of it, a Hugh Moore smoking jacket.

'Owen!' Jiffy or Jilly or whoever the bangs girl was exclaimed. She turned a deep red shade that matched her lip gloss. Owen smiled. *Way to still have it, Carlyle.*

'Thanks for stopping by,' Jack said in a sultry voice. She eased over, realizing her thigh was partially stuck to the cracked red vinyl booth. Gross. They'd definitely have to step up their hangout locations this year. It was absurd to go to a fancy dinner still smelling like someone else's onion rings.

'No problem.' Owen tugged at his blue button-down uncomfortably and shifted from side to side. Normally, he'd have asked Avery if he looked okay, but things had been awkward between them since Friday. Besides, his wardrobe was the *least* of his concerns tonight.

'So, you guys are going on a double date?' Genevieve raised an eyebrow and took a sip of her black coffee. 'That sounds so quaint. Where are you going?'

'2Na. You know, that new Morimoto-style place downtown? It just opened a few weeks ago.' Jack shrugged, trying to look blasé even though she was kind of excited about their night out on the town. And of course, having her handsome 'boyfriend' go out of his way to pick her up would give her bragging rights with her friends for weeks. She fished inside her bright orange Hermès wallet to throw down a few dollars for whatever the fuck they'd eaten. She felt totally piggish, but she'd never been the type of girl who could subsist on sushi alone.

'I've got it,' Owen offered gallantly, pulling out a crisp twenty from his pocket and throwing it on the cracked dishwater-colored linoleum table. He sort of liked showing off in front of Jack's friends. Maybe there was something to this whole dating thing, even though, strictly speaking, this evening with Jack would be the first official 'date' he'd ever been on.

Let's raise our crappy diner mugs to new experiences.

'Thanks, Owen!' Jiffy giggled ridiculously. Jack sighed. Even though she loved her friends, when they were all together they invariably turned into a group of giggly girls.

Jack and Owen walked out onto the pavement, crowded with commuters hurrying home. Jack took his hand. 'I thought we could walk. It's such a nice night.' She swung her large blue bag over her other arm.

Owen felt her thin fingers laced in his as they headed down Madison. The sun was setting and he had to squint. He couldn't believe that soon it'd be dark at this time of night.

'What are you thinking about?' Jack questioned. She looked at him with her pointed chin upturned, as if she really did want to know.

'Nothing.' Owen sighed in contentment. But then, as he remembered where they were headed, he felt a slice of fear run up his stomach. He *really* didn't want to see Kelsey. Or Rhys. Or, more specifically, Kelsey and Rhys *together*.

'Hold on, can we stop here for a second?' Jack asked. They were standing by a large tower complex with interlocking gold *C*'s out front. She knelt down and adjusted the strap of her peep-toe heels.

Jack pretended to fiddle with her Louboutins and then straightened, resisting the urge to grab Owen and kiss him for J.P.'s viewing pleasure. Instead, she grabbed his arm and held it tightly. But as she stole a glance at J.P.'s window dozens of stories above, she realized the absurdity of orchestrating a make-out session on the off chance her ex-boyfriend would even be at home right now. 'Never mind,' she muttered, taking his hand back in hers.

'So, where is this place?' Owen asked as they continued walking south. He was still sort of fuzzy with his Manhattan geography, but was pretty sure Soho wasn't walkable from the Upper East Side.

Says Mr I Do Triathlons for Fun!

'It's far,' Jack admitted. 'We should probably take a cab. I just thought it'd be nice to get some fresh air,' she fibbed.

She squinted her freckle-surrounded eyes uptown and expertly lifted her arm to hail a cab. Immediately one screeched to the curb. Owen and Jack climbed in, and Owen was surprised by how close Jack sat to him. They awkwardly watched the news broadcast on the tiny backseat television. Today was the last day of summer, the announcer noted.

'It'll be cold soon.' Owen gestured at the screen. Jack

nodded, her face in profile reminding him of those Greek statues in the Met.

Finally, the cab screeched to a halt in front of a garish orange, red, and blue restaurant on a cobblestoned side street. A long line of well-dressed people snaked into the overcrowded lobby.

'Uh, we have a reservation? I think it's under Sterling?' Owen asked the clipboard-wielding hostess tentatively as they entered.

'Who *is* that? He's hot!' a girl behind them whispered in admiration. Owen smiled awkwardly.

'The rest of the party isn't here.' The hostess smiled. 'Would you mind waiting at the bar?' She winked at Owen.

Owen escorted Jack over to the bar and instantaneously, two saketinis appeared in front of them.

'Here's to first dates,' she said, raising her glass. Owen smiled. Jack was really pretty, but she also seemed to have a good sense of humor about the whole situation. He clinked his glass with hers and took a swig. And then he looked up from the lime bobbing in his drink to see Kelsey, in a lime green patterned dress with pink flowers. On anyone else, it would have looked ridiculous, but Kelsey looked like she was coming from a vacation hut on some fabulously remote tropical island. Owen's stomach flip-flopped and he slammed his empty purple glass on the shiny black wood bar harder than he'd intended.

Jack looked up. She watched as Owen's eyes flicked over Kelsey's body, barely registering Rhys standing behind her.

'Hi,' Jack said authoritatively in Kelsey's general direction. She was trying hard not to be bitchy, though of course she'd noticed Kelsey's ridiculously casual dress. And she'd sort of gone overboard on that whole enamel accessory trend, wearing about five bracelets on each wrist.

Not like she was judging.

'Table's ready,' their waiter said. He instantly rolled his eyes when he took in their teenage double date. He'd clearly assumed the reservation was for *Lady* Sterling, not her son. They were escorted to a ridiculously tiny black booth in the corner and offered a bottle of sake.

'Hi, I'm Owen. Nice to see you again.' Owen offered his hand to Kelsey, feeling ridiculous as they all crowded into the booth. The booths were separated by sheer white curtains, embroidered with elaborate flowers and butterflies. With the curtain closed, it sort of felt like they were in one of those old-fashioned train cars from a movie like *Murder on the Orient Express*. It would be really romantic on a date, but for this occasion it just felt like torture.

'I've heard a lot about you,' Kelsey said, playing with the chopsticks sitting on her black enamel plate. The way she said it wasn't bitchy, exactly, but her tone sent a shiver of fear up Owen's spine. She sounded like she really didn't care, like she was meeting any asshole member of the swim team and she'd be nice, but not any nicer than she had to be. Owen pounded down his saketini and reached for the bottle of sake.

'Who wants some?' he offered, holding up the bottle. He didn't look at Kelsey. Or Jack. Or Rhys.

'Sure,' Rhys said affably. 'So, I was telling Kelsey that you're from Nantucket. Her family has a house on the Cape.'

'It's totally different,' Kelsey and Owen said at the same time.

'Sorry,' Owen quickly apologized. Kelsey shook her head and sighed heavily, as if Owen had just exploded in a string of swear words. Owen tugged the collar of his shirt. He looked at the curtain again, suddenly reminded of the Sartre play *No Exit*, which they'd read in French class last year. In the play, three characters find themselves in hell, tortured only by one another. It was sort of how he felt right now. Whenever Kelsey looked at him with that awful expression of indifference and disgust, he felt a little stab in his chest. And yet, he couldn't *stop* looking at her. It was utter torment.

'So, how are you, Jack?' Rhys tried to start a conversation again, grasping at straws. He smiled at the redheaded, freckle-faced girl. She and Owen looked good together, but something just seemed . . . off. And he didn't know why Kelsey, who was usually so friendly, was being so standoffish to Owen.

'Are you okay?' Rhys whispered to Kelsey. She was looking down at her fingernails.

'I'm really happy I'm here with you,' Kelsey whispered, loudly enough for Owen and Jack to hear. Rhys gulped his glass of sake, which burned his throat. He wasn't really sure what Kelsey meant. She almost sounded angry, but when he turned again to look into her eyes, she had an eager smile pasted on her face. Weird.

'This is a nice place,' he commented desperately, looking at the random sculpture of a tiger set up on a ledge above Owen's head. It looked like it was ready to attack.

Just like some members of the dinner party.

The waiter whisked open the curtain and looked at all of them, disappointed that he hadn't caught them making out under the table or doing something completely inappropriate so he could kick them out. 'Compliments of the chef.' He set down a plate of steaming edamame. The small green nubs reminded Owen of the praying mantises that were always in their garden in Nantucket. 'Ready to order?' the waiter asked brusquely.

Owen consulted the menu, suddenly not feeling hungry at all. It didn't matter. Rhys was rattling off dishes as if he were freaking Japanese. Owen smiled tightly and noticed Kat's hand on Rhys's knee. He felt like he was going to be sick.

'Got it,' the waiter huffed as Rhys finished his elaborate order, and closed the curtains again.

'Are you okay?' Jack whispered in Owen's ear.

'Yeah.' Owen nodded as he grabbed a piece of edamame. Rhys now had his hand on Kelsey's shoulder and was edging his fingers underneath the straps of her sundress. Owen abruptly reached over for Jack's hand but accidentally tipped over her glass.

'Sorry,' he apologized, dabbing lamely at the countertop with a thick cloth napkin. He felt like a jerk.

'It's fine.' Jack shrugged. Surprisingly, she wasn't even put out by the small droplets landing in a starlike pattern on her black Vivienne Tam cocktail dress. Something about the candlelight, the dark curtains, and the fact that Rhys and Kelsey were totally ignoring them made it feel like they were in a romantic world of their own.

The alcohol didn't hurt either.

Owen was hardly breathing, trying to listen to Rhys and Kelsey's conversation. Their fingers were intertwined, and Kelsey's silvery blue eyes looked almost wet. Was she crying? As if on cue, Kelsey glanced over and glared at Owen.

'Did you want to say something?' she asked pointedly. Suddenly, everyone was staring at him. Owen felt his ears turn red.

'No . . . actually, I think I have to leave.' Owen shrugged apologetically as he fumbled in his pocket. He knew it was abrupt and antisocial, but he just couldn't be here anymore. He pulled out his iPhone. 'It's . . . my sisters. They're having some type of problem,' Owen finished lamely, hoping they'd buy the family emergency story.

'Okay, man,' Rhys looked concerned. 'Jack, you can definitely feel free to stay,' he offered generously.

Jack smiled grimly at Owen's retreating back, barely acknowledging Rhys's lame attempt at politesse. She'd have to give Owen a stern talking-to later. What the fuck was that all about? She'd forgotten what a pain in the ass having a boyfriend could be.

Has she also forgotten he's not actually her boyfriend?

clothes call

'Miss, this is a private club!' A man wearing a three-piece suit rushed out from behind a mahogany desk. Baby stopped mid-walk and looked around in confusion. Atlas, 3 East Sixtieth Street. She *thought* that was the address J.P. had given her. She was supposed to meet him and his parents at the club for dinner tonight, but maybe she'd gotten the numbers wrong. She rooted through her green vinyl Brooklyn Industries bag for the piece of paper where she'd written the address.

'Sorry, I thought I was meeting someone here. This is the Atlas Club?' Baby wore an oversize red and black Alive + Olivia tunic dress she'd found in Avery's closet. It was large on her tiny frame, so she'd belted it with one of Edie's old hippie-leather belts, and added a few necklaces and bracelets. Fur-clad ladies and tuxedoed men milled around the lobby. A harp and a violin played in the background. She definitely did not fit in.

Again.

'You're quite sure you're meeting your party here?' The guy knitted his bushy salt-and-pepper eyebrows together. He had a tiny mustache that looked like the offspring of his out-of-control eyebrows. Normally, Baby would have found it funny, but right now she was just annoyed. Who was he to tell her that she didn't belong here? Baby narrowed her eyes at him.

'There you are!'

Baby whirled around and saw J.P. dressed in an impeccable gray suit, trailed by his flashy real-estate developer dad and his former European supermodel mom. A cowboy hat covered Dick Cashman's Pepto-Bismol-colored bald head and Tatyana Cashman's low-cut black-and-white shirt only enhanced her voluminous cleavage.

'Well, look what the cat dragged in!' Dick clapped his hand against Baby's back, almost causing her to lose her balance. She started coughing at the overwhelming cloud of spicy perfume following Tatyana.

'Great to see you.' Baby smiled.

'Mr Cashman,' the club's host said reverentially and stepped back.

'How are you?' Dick pumped the man's hand up and down so hard a blue vein throbbed in his temple. 'They treatin' you well? You look a little exhausted. Tell you what, I have a bunch of new casinos out in Vegas. You come out there, play some poker, bring a lady friend, she can see one of those old broad's concerts, it'll be great,' Dick announced grandly with a twinkle in his eye. Tatyana wandered off to the large gilt-encrusted mirror set up in the corner and began reapplying her dark lipstick.

'Sir, I . . . Thank you,' the host said, clearly flustered.

'So, I guess I'll bring the gang up to the usual spot? Baby, you've got to try the venison here. Tastes like fucking Bambi. Oh, right, you like to cuddle animals.' Dick shook his head in sorrow.

'No, I eat everything,' Baby said easily. Like many people, Dick Cashman assumed that her bohemian look meant she was a vegetarian.

'Mr Cashman, sir . . .' The host shifted uncomfortably.

'Come on, we're all friends here – call me Dick!' His voice rang through the lobby just as the harpist stopped playing.

'Dick, then,' the host said, blushing red and motioning for him to come closer to him. 'You're one of the most loyal and generous members of the club, and, as you know, we love meeting all your friends and family.' He glanced meaningfully at the LV carrier hanging from Tatyana's fleshy arm that contained one of the Cashman's three dogs. 'However, as you also know, we're a club based on standards, and I'm afraid the young master's guest simply is not dressed for the occasion. But, of course, if you'd like, you could sit at the bar, or the young miss could run home and change . . .' he said discreetly. Baby turned red. She felt like she was in *Pretty Woman*, when Julia Roberts, the hooker with a heart of gold, gets kicked out of a Rodeo Drive boutique. Next to her, J.P. was awkwardly shuffling from foot to Gucci loafer-clad foot.

'Nonsense, we can eat at the bar. Closer to the booze! Come on!' Dick roared. He sidled up to Tatyana, squeezing her enormous ass. It was encased in a pencil-thin Prada skirt that *only* looked good on prepubescent European models.

'Sorry about that. I can go home and we can meet up later.' Baby shrugged as they entered the elevator, which was run by a million-year-old attendant. A dress code? It was one thing for school, but for a restaurant to be so strict just seemed absurd.

'No, it's fine. It's my fault, I should have told you.' J. P. furrowed his brow in concern and squeezed her hand harder. They entered the bar area, where they sat down in a line.

'Four Glenfiddiches on the rocks,' Dick called gallantly. 'Scotch always fixes everything. And the menus. And, hey, do you have any of those bar snacks?'

Although the room was dark, with brocade curtains, it was still light outside, and Baby could see the corner of Central Park out the window. Horses and carriages were gathered along Central Park South, and runners paused on the corner, stretching. Baby sighed. She felt like she needed to run.

'You okay, really?' J.P. asked in concern as two heavy glass tumblers were planted in front of them, followed by pesto- and prosciutto-layered mini sandwiches. Baby guessed those were the bar snacks. They were a far cry from the days-old Chex mix at the Upper West Side pub she'd gone to with Sydney. She took one of the elaborately constructed sandwiches and nibbled on the corner.

'My dad loves it here. You know that old Marx brothers joke, "I won't be a member of any clubs that'll have me"? My dad is the opposite. He belongs to, like, every club in the city,' J.P. babbled. Baby forced a smile. Maybe J. P. was nervous around his parents, but he sounded like he was trying to impress a golfing buddy. She squeezed his hand again, then pointed at a lady in the next room who held a drink in each of her hands and leaned against the piano for support. She looked like she was ready to break out into song at any moment, and at a place like this, Baby wondered if anybody would be able to stop her. J.P. cracked a wide grin and shook his head. Baby ate the rest of her sandwich, relieved. It was just J.P. Her boyfriend. So, yeah, he had grown up in this life of ridiculous excess, but who was she to judge? She'd grown up sleeping outside, with a mom who hosted weeklong bacchanalia parties on the beach. In a way, it was sort of the same thing.

Minus the private clubs, private helicopters, and private investments.

'Well, I'm going to get the venison,' Dick announced to the bar. 'Shall we just get it for everyone? And some more drinks. Surprise us.' Dick tipped his cowboy hat jovially at the bartender.

Because of course, cowboy hats are part of the dress code.

'So, Baby, vat are you vearing to zee party on Saturday?' Tatyana asked, pursing her platypuslike lips. She leaned in so close that Baby had to swerve to avoid getting Chanel lipstick smeared all over her cheek.

'I don't know yet.' Baby shrugged. She hadn't really thought about what she was going to wear to the swim team dinner, even though it was tomorrow night. Benefits in Nantucket were either on the beach or in the firehouse.

'Maybe we could go shopping togezzer. But ze problem is you are so skinny! Eat, eat!' Tatyana pushed another sandwich toward Baby, who hastily accepted it. If she didn't, J.P.'s mom would probably end up feeding it to her. Tatyana sneaked two sandwiches into the carrier and the dog let out a low growl. 'Eez settled then.' She turned back to Baby. 'We shop for ze perfect dress for you tomorrow.'

'No, don't worry about it . . .' Baby trailed off. She

imagined herself with Tatyana Cashman as her stylist. By the end of the day she'd be wearing dark lipstick and ass-tight gold pants.

'Why not go with her? It would be nice to get a new dress.' J.P. leaned in to whisper in Baby's ear. 'You guys would have fun.'

Have fun? Baby's smile faltered. Since when did Shopping for Party Dresses + Baby Carlyle = Fun? Didn't he know her at all? And even if she did get barred from fancy private clubs for being a little, well, *unique*, wasn't that what he liked about her?

'Okay, thanks, that'd be great,' Baby mumbled, picking at a new appetizer that had appeared, a tasteless lump of gelatinous substance that looked like tree bark. Tatyana nodded appreciatively, happy to be of service.

'Well, now that that's settled, I'm takin' my lady for a hoedown!' Dick pulled Tatyana up and over toward the dance floor. They swayed to some old-school Frank Sinatra. It was really cute, in a way, and Baby knew J.P.'s parents meant well – and so did J.P. She felt her Nokia against her hip and willed herself *not* to think about what fun things Sydney, Mateo, or any of the other URs were up to right now.

'You know what'd be really fun?' Baby whispered to J. P., suddenly inspired. She took another swig of scotch and wiped the back of her mouth with her hand. 'What if we made a pact that wherever we were, whenever it happened, if one of us called each other and decided to go to . . . oh, I don't know, Barcelona, we'd take the next plane out. Nothing except passports. What do you think?' Baby bounced up and down on the thick cushion of the bar stool in excitement.

'Just . . . go?' J.P. asked in confusion. 'What about school?'

'Write a report about it! Come on! Live a little. Not *now*,' she added. 'But sometime soon. When I call you. Or when you call me.' Baby's eyes searched J.P.'s. He *had* to say yes. Behind them, Dick was groping Tatyana's ass, their dinner apparently forgotten, as the piano player played 'Strangers in the Night.'

'I'm in,' J.P. finally said, his face breaking into a smile. Baby smiled back in relief. She could hardly wait to *experience* the world, especially with her boyfriend by her side.

'*Salud!*' J.P. added randomly. It meant *cheers* in Spanish. He held up his glass and Baby joyfully clinked it with hers.

Salud indeed.

![lips logo] **gossipgirl.net** Disclaimer: All the real names of places, people, and events have been altered or abbreviated to protect the innocent. Namely, me.

| topics | sightings | your e-mail | post a question |

hey people!

ready to benefit?

It's the first big party of the season. The annual St Jude's swim team benefit may officially benefit those less fortunate – technically, the proceeds go to buying public schools pool time at the Y – but with a date auction that pretty much *encourages* hooking up, it really benefits all of us. It's become a fall tradition, the kickoff to mischief, the official nod that in between studying for AP tests and participating in every extracurricular activity possible, we ought to put down the books, take off the uniforms, kick up our heels, and *misbehave.* Since it's for charity, don't be shy about raising your paddle high for that butterflyer with the killer shoulders or the cutie you want to personally tutor you in the breaststroke. But for the newbies, remember: this is a school-sponsored event. Meaning? Get your flasks ready and be prepared to flip the sober switch at a moment's notice. You never know when an adult will wander over to the young and fun tables to 'bond.' Don't say I didn't warn you!

With that in mind, it's come to my attention that there have been more than a few etiquette breaches lately. While I don't want to sound old-fashioned, it's in all of our best interests not to totally embarrass ourselves at the first big event of the year. To help, here's a handy reminder of proper behavior.

No texting under the table. Instead, go the infinitely more romantic and Henry James–ian route of sending your potential hookup a note through the waiter. Bonus if your note is *to* the waiter.

Dress appropriately. *With panties.* In addition, gentlemen, even if your date is wearing a cleavage-baring Chloé dress whose bejeweled straps 'accidentally' slide down, you do not have permission to stare at her chest.

Remember **the golden rule of drinking**: one drink per hour, maximum, and please drink one glass of Pellegrino for every flute of Veuve. As if any of us can keep track.

So roll this list up and stick it in your cigarette case. Or smoke it. Good parties happen only when you break the rules!

sightings

A setting up camp at Serafina on Sixty-first and Madison, nursing her third cappuccino with a line of boys out the door. Interviewing prospects for the benefit? **B** shopping with **J.P.**'s mom, at Barneys. And Bergdorf's. And Bloomingdale's. Oh dear. Let's hope they have something to show for it that isn't too shiny and stretchy! **O**, looking a little sad, as he ran around the Central Park Reservoir over and over again. Building up his endurance for tonight? **J**, **S.J.**, and **G** standing outside the Ninety-second Street Y. Hoping to get some early bidding in, ladies?

your e-mail

 Dear Gossip Girl,

I work at an exclusive Fifth Avenue salon, and this afternoon, we had a bunch of very attractive gentlemen come in for a waxing session – everything off, including facial hair. They look so good, we're offering a special on waxing for men.

I know everyone reads you, so I thought I would enlist you to pass on the message.

– Wax 4 Less

A: Dear Wax 4 Less,

Hallelujah, and can I speak for the ladies of the Upper East Side when I say, not a moment too soon? Boys who didn't get the memo? Consider this your final warning to ditch the facial hair and any other unsightly hair in unmentionable places.

– GG

a final etiquette note

One of the huge attractions of a party is the potential to meet the mate of your dreams. And, when you do, you naturally want to get to know them. *Really* get to know them. But no matter what corner you find – whether it's under a table, in an elevator, or in the bed of the host's parents – it's *never* as private as you think. So proceed with caution. Someone is always watching. And not just me.

See you all at the benefit!

You know you love me.

picture perfect

'Ladies first.' Tristan St Clair held the black door of the sleek town car open for Avery. She grinned hugely, almost sad that they had reached their destination: the high-rise Delancey, a brand-new Lower East Side boutique hotel, which stood out among the walk-up brick buildings surrounding it. A royal blue mat with a pattern of gold scripted *D*'s covered the sidewalk, and three doormen stood in rapt attention. It was all too *perfect*.

Isn't that someone else's word?

Tristan was just as cute as his photographs, and was luckily home in Manhattan for the weekend from Buckhead, a private school in Pennsylvania. He had arrived at the Carlyle penthouse to pick her up in his parents' town car, which was stocked with bottles of chilled champagne. They had toasted each other as the car raced downtown, talking about his captainship of the Buckhead squash team and her love of New York City. They'd even made tentative plans to spend Sunday at the Met, since Avery hadn't had a chance to actually go *in* since she'd moved to the city.

'I heard she had to pay this guy, like, five hundred dollars an hour to come here. She got a discount because he's, like, the great-great-grandson of one of those Constance overseer ladies or something. Hopefully it's her own money and not Constance's, you know?' Chelsy Chapin, a pug-nosed sophomore whispered to Elisabeth Cort, an unfortunately truck-shaped junior, as Avery breezed into the Delancey with Tristan on her arm.

'Hi there.' Avery greeted them and handed over her invitation. She could tell from the way they instantly blushed they had been talking about her. Well, who cared? *They* were the dateless ones taking invites, hunkered down on the strawberry jam–colored love seat in the lobby. She felt Tristan's strong arm guide the small of her back and she felt all jittery inside, a feeling she usually only got when she drank too many iced coffees from Dean & DeLuca.

It was so *nice* to have a boyfriend, Avery thought as he escorted her to the elevator.

Boyfriend? Easy there, tiger!

As the elevator whooshed up to the twenty-third floor, Avery could barely control the butterflies in her stomach. She examined her reflection in the elevator's mirrored surface. She loved how she only came up to Tristan's chin. She'd always been tall, and tonight she was wearing four-inch Viktor & Rolf maroon slingbacks that perfectly matched her Stella McCartney cashmere knit short-sleeved dress. Which meant Tristan was *really* tall. She felt even more nervous than she had on her first day at Constance. Finally, with Tristan at her side, she was going to prove to the rest of her classmates that she wasn't some freaky, backward, small-town girl. She was Avery Carlyle, a girl boys would do anything for.

Tell 'em, sister!

'You look beautiful,' Tristan murmured into Avery's

freshly washed, gleaming blond hair – courtesy of her stylist Nico at Oscar Blandi salon. Then he sneezed.

'Excuse me.' He frowned as he pulled a brilliant white handkerchief out of his pocket and discreetly dabbed his nose. A handkerchief? Avery tried to conceal her enthusiasm. How grown up and sophisticated!

'You know, I have to admit I was a little nervous when Grandmother Muffy set this up. Sometimes she can be a little bit . . . eccentric,' Tristan commented as they navigated around the large round tables set up throughout the high-ceilinged event space. *But?* Avery's heart pounded faster.

'Truffle oil–infused free-range chicken dumplings?' An overzealous, totally bald waiter thrust a steaming silver platter in front of them. Avery wrinkled her nose and practically pushed the platter away. Her stomach was growling, but she'd deal with that later. She needed to know what Tristan thought of her.

'You were saying?' Avery asked sweetly, hoping she didn't sound too obvious. She pushed a stray lock of hair behind her ear and gazed into Tristan's blue eyes and nervously bit her MAC-glossed bottom lip.

'Has anyone told you how beautiful you are?' Tristan asked, holding both of her hands and gazing into her blue eyes. Avery felt herself melt. Tristan sneezed again and Avery raised a just-plucked eyebrow in concern. Could he be sick? She imagined him coming down with consumption, or whatever that disease was lovers always seemed to contract in nineteenth-century operas. She'd valiantly attempt to nurse him back to health on top of some mountain, staying strong for her one true love. Then, after he died, she could start a foundation for him and throw fabulous parties, wearing elegant all-black gowns with a lace veil.

'Sorry.' Tristan shook his head ruefully. 'It's just my allergies. I guess we should find our table.'

'Hey!' Baby came up to them, poking Avery hard under the ribs. Avery took in her seven-minutes-younger sister. Even though she'd seen her getting dressed in the apartment, seeing Baby in public, next to an impeccably dressed J. P. Cashman, was stunning. Avery hadn't seen her so dressed up since they were ten and Grandmother Avery had taken them to Easter services at Park Avenue Episcopal Church. Baby wore a white Rodarte dress with black chiffon flowers sewn onto it, and looked like an elegant woodland sprite. Avery peered down and noticed that despite her couture dress Baby was still wearing her favorite pair of dirty white Havaiana flip-flops.

Some things never change.

J.P. looked incredible in a crisp custom-made steel gray Brooks Brothers suit. Normally Avery would have felt a little jealous at the sight of her hippie sister on the arm of the Upper East Side's most eligible bachelor, but now, with Tristan's strong, squash-callused hand resting protectively on her hip, she simply smiled.

'I found our table – number nineteen. Owen and She-Who-Shall-Not-Be-Named are holding seats for us.' Baby rolled her large brown eyes. 'I thought we'd give them the private couple time they like so much.' Avery smiled. Baby was being completely sarcastic, but since she sounded so sweet, no one would even bat an eye.

They wandered over to the table, where Owen was staring intently at the tablecloth. In a sky blue Hermès tie that perfectly matched his intense blue eyes, he looked dapper and handsome. No *wonder* all the girls were looking at him. Still, Owen seemed in his own world, while Jack was happily chatting away with Owen's friend, Rhys Sterling, and his girlfriend.

'You look nice, Ave,' Owen mumbled. He nodded at Tristan, who was standing close beside her. 'Hey,' he said by way of boy-greeting.

'Thanks,' Avery replied in what she hoped was an ice queen–type voice. She glared at Jack, but she didn't look up. Around them, people were shuffling to their tables, including Edie, who had come to the hotel straight from an art opening. She wore a pink and blue sari, her hair pulled up in chopsticks, and was gesticulating wildly, in deep conversation with a bored-looking businessman. Owen and Avery caught each other's eye and smiled at the same time. Avery felt her heart soften toward her brother a little bit. Maybe it wasn't so bad that he was dating the Antichrist. At least now Jack could see up close how *not* single Avery was. Avery leaned in toward Tristan.

Just then, a photographer stepped up.

'I'm Bill, from the *New York Times*. Would you ladies mind?' Avery smiled fakely as she, Kelsey, Jack, and Baby huddled in close. 'Beautiful! You're the flowers of the Upper East Side,' the photographer commented as he snapped away.

Just watch out for the thorns.

Avery couldn't resist digging her manicured nails *just slightly* into Jack's alabaster skin as they squeezed together shoulder to shoulder.

Smile!

They pulled away and sat back down at the table. An awkward silence ensued.

Owen looked helplessly from Avery and Tristan to Rhys and Kelsey to Baby and J.P. to Jack. He could practically taste the tension at the table. Rhys was delicately feeding Kelsey a fried olive from a platter. 'Anyone want a drink?' Owen asked lamely. Elaborate mocktails with fun names like the Fizzy Mermaid and the Slippery Seal were being passed around by overeager waiters. The mocktails were only tolerable because everyone invited knew the drill and had brought their own alcohol of choice. Owen wished he'd brought a whole bottle instead of a flask. Anything to make him stop caring about Rhys and Kelsey touching each other.

'I'll have one, thank you.' Jack smiled and touched Owen's arm, bringing him back to reality. She was wearing a delicate-looking chestnut brown dress, her hair swept up in a complicated style, a few strands of her silky auburn hair falling to her shoulders.

'Here.' Owen surreptitiously poured a generous swig of Maker's Mark from his flask into her Diet Coke.

'Thanks.' Jack noticed that Avery and Mr Perfect Prep School Boy's hands were intertwined under the table. Avery looked like her brother, so well scrubbed, as if nothing bad had ever happened to her. Meanwhile, J.P. and Baby had inched away from the table and were standing by one of the large picture windows, looking down in awe, as if they were seeing a fireworks display instead of dirty former tenement houses. Jack fought the urge to stand up and scream. She wanted to do *something* to pull them out of their oh-so-fucking-happy reverie. She hoped J.P. had gotten lice or some other tragically embarrassing communicable pest from Baby, who, Jack realized, didn't look dirty or hippieish at all tonight.

She felt small tears prick her eyes and angrily brushed them away. Hello, at least she wasn't at the single-girl table. She was fine. Perfect, even. She drained her glass and slammed it down on the white tablecloth.

'You look beautiful,' Owen whispered into her ear. Jack could hear a sense of urgency in his voice, and knew he was trying to block out the disgusting Rhys and Kelsey PDA occurring across the table. She turned toward Owen, and, almost in a trance, pressed her lips against his. His mouth tasted minty and clean, and his teeth were smooth like porcelain. Owen's lips were still for a second, as if locked in surprise, but then moved against hers eagerly.

Jack pulled back when she heard J.P.'s familiar throat clearing half-cough. He pulled the chair out next to her, making a loud scraping sound, and he and Baby eased back into their seats. *Take that, fuckfaces,* Jack thought victoriously. She gave a slight shrug and turned back to Owen. She was surprised at how much she enjoyed kissing him. Owen took another swig of his drink, smiling slightly, the tips of his ears faintly pink.

'Excuse me everyone.' The guys' swim coach stood up from a center table and tapped a microphone. It let out a loud screech of feedback, and the two hundred guests covered their ears. His tuxedo shirt was unbuttoned to show six inches of perfectly hairless, gleaming chest, and his reddish brown hair was spiked at uneven angles. He sort of looked like a greased baby duck.

Jack turned back to J.P., who was whispering into Baby's ear. Baby's head was thrown back, and her tiny teeth were gleaming. She wondered what J.P. was saying that was so funny. Telling fucking knock-knock jokes? Jack stared at a point above J.P.'s eyes. It was a trick she'd learned in ballet, to make sure her partner was looking at her right before a leap or a tour jeté. She waited for J.P.'s eyes to flick away from Baby's delicate mouth. As soon as she knew she had his attention, she turned to Owen, took his chin in her hand, and kissed him again, harder and more passionately this time. If all the world was a stage, she was putting on the performance of a lifetime.

Who's acting?

love is in the air . . . among other things

'So, are we actually going to bid? And do they take AmEx?' Jiffy asked, brushing her long brown bangs out of her eyes. The dinner plates had been cleared away, the lights were dimmed, the music was turned up, and most parents had already written generous checks to support the cause and left to continue their evenings at the Met.

'No, we're going to *donate*. It's for charity. It's not like we're buying dates, you know? We're donating to charity,' Genevieve said defensively, taking a long swig from her pee-colored drink that was obviously a heavily vodka-infused Fizzy Mermaid.

Avery paused en route from the bar for tonic waters when she heard her former friends. She almost felt sorry for them, bidding on dates.

Key word: *almost*.

Whatever. Ignoring them, she marched back to her table, where Tristan already stood with her chair pulled out.

'Thank you!' Avery paused and rummaged through the small black vintage Prada clutch she'd inherited from Grandmother Avery. At home she had a photograph of

Grandmother Avery holding it at a White House Christmas party, laughing with Jackie Kennedy. You could just make out Marilyn Monroe pouting jealously at them from the corner. Avery had brought the purse as a good luck charm, but even she couldn't believe how smoothly the night was going. She pulled out a small travel-size Creed Love in White purse spray and gently sprayed it behind her ears, inhaling the scent of oranges and sandalwood. She was reminded of an Estée Lauder quote her grandmother had once relayed to her: 'Perfume is like love – you can never get enough.' She spritzed a tiny bit more on her collarbone.

'Stop!' She heard Tristan's panicked voice. Oh. Did *he* want to spray it on her? She paused and passed him the tiny vial. She wanted tonight to be all about love. After all, she could see her and Tristan together forever: they'd have a huge wedding in St Patrick's, followed by a honeymoon in Capri, and then they'd settle into a town house just like Grandmother Avery's . . .

Her reverie was interrupted by an enormous, spit-spraying sneeze.

'Oh my God,' Tristan exclaimed. His eyes were red and there was a look of shock on his face. He quickly thrust his hand in his pocket, pulled out a large pink tablet, and threw it in his mouth, gulping down an entire glass of water. Avery paused in concern.

'Are you okay?' she asked. Was he doing *drugs*? Why did something have to be defective with every guy she tried to date?

And why isn't there such a thing as a boyfriend warranty?

Tristan sneezed again, even more forcefully than before.

Small droplets of yellow snot landed on the tablecloth. Across the table, Baby looked like she was going to explode with giggles. Avery gave her a death stare.

'Are you okay? What's wrong?' Avery repeated in concern. She realized that everyone, including the coach, was looking at them.

'Is table nineteen all right, or do they need a moment?' Coach Siegel practically yelled into the microphone. 'I have to say, folks, that's the effect my star swimmers, Rhys and Owen, have on a table.' A well of polite laughter rippled through the audience.

'Owen's my boy!' Avery heard her mother's distinctive voice, followed by her signature wolf whistle.

'We're fine,' Tristan choked, sneezing again. Avery tried to move her chair several inches away without being obvious.

'Just *fine*,' she repeated, and turned her full attention back to the program.

'Okay, people, now that everything has settled down, we're going to begin our date auction. Once these swimmers are in season, I won't let them see any ladies, so enjoy them while they're hot. And, remember, it's all for charity.' Coach leered at the audience. 'Don't forget, ladies, I'm single too. I'll be taking bids *after* this portion of the evening is over.' He licked his lips suggestively and turned away from the microphone to grab the scrawny arm of Chadwick Jenkins. Dressed in a black suit and purple tie, he looked like he'd been outfitted by Calvin Klein Kids. He stood nervously, shifting from one foot to the other, squinting around the room.

Tristan sneezed again, making a noise that sounded like a seal coming up for air.

'Is that a bid?' Coach looked over at their table and Avery felt herself turn bright red. Tristan shook his head and put his napkin over his mouth and face. Great. Now he looked like he was about to rob a bank.

'Twenty dollars?' a scrawny girl who was probably Chadwick's little sister squeaked as she raised her paddle. One of the swim team guys hooted.

'Fifty.' Hugh Moore held up his paddle with a bored gesture, a wicked grin spreading across his face.

'Okay, we have fifty.' Coach's eyes gleamed as his beady eyes scanned the room to see if any women were watching. Avery took the pause to tap Tristan hard on the bicep. He turned to her, his face bright red, as if he'd just run a 10K. That was it. If he was dying, he might as well do it in the lobby. She pulled him out of his seat and dragged him around the perimeter of the room, all too aware that every eye was on her.

'Anyone else? We've got fifty dollars for Chadwick,' Coach announced as all eyes turned back to the terrified-looking ninth grader.

'Aw, yeah, slave! Just *wait* until you clean out my locker,' Avery heard Hugh cheering. Ugh. She'd pay fifty dollars to get rid of Sneezy right about now.

'What's wrong?' Avery demanded as soon as they left the ballroom and stood in the pink-wallpapered anteroom.

'AH-CHOO!' Tristan sneezed again, and then three more times. He leaned against the wall for balance as he dragged the back of his hand under his nose.

Um, ew?

'It's you.' He shook his head ruefully. 'Oh no, I mean, it's not *you*, you're beautiful,' he backtracked. He sneezed again, a thin arc of green snot landing dangerously close to Avery's dress. 'Oh my God, I thought I was over this,' he exclaimed. He held out his hand as if to touch Avery's shoulder, but she backed away, narrowing her eyes in suspicion. She could not *believe* her date had turned out to be a biohazard.

'It's your perfume.' He sneezed again. 'And those flowers.' He nodded at the thin glass bowls of delicate orchids on the cocktail tables around the room. 'I'm sorry. I should probably call my allergist. Are you still up for the Met tomorrow?' he asked. Avery saw a hopeful glint in his runny blue eyes, but she shook her head firmly. She wasn't *that* desperate. Tristan hurried away, sneezing the whole time.

Avery watched his broad, retreating back and sighed heavily. She sniffed her wrist. Maybe she exuded some type of undiscovered pheromone that repelled men.

She walked over to a window and looked out at Manhattan. The buildings seemed to wink back at her mockingly. How come whenever she got so close to living her New York City dream, everything fell apart? She sighed. She knew that she should hold her chin high and march back into the auction, but somehow, she couldn't. Instead, she turned toward the elevator and pressed the gold button again and again until the elevator doors slid mercifully open. She might as well just go back to her apartment and never leave again.

Inside, the auction was rolling on and the guests were getting even more rowdy. Even the parents who'd stayed were whooping every time a girl raised her bid on one of the swimmers. Jack wondered where Avery had run off to, and why her boyfriend had seemed to be allergic to her. But she had more important things to attend to. She clutched her wallet nervously. Owen was next to be auctioned off, and, as his date, she was sort of required to bid on him. She hoped he wasn't too expensive, but then again, who wanted something cheap?

A true conundrum.

'Okay, these two gentlemen lead the team, so I'm going to put them head-to-head,' Coach jovially announced. 'A little friendly competition to toughen them up.'

He has *no* idea.

Owen glanced sideways at Rhys as he shuffled from foot to foot. Except for practice, he'd barely seen Rhys over the last few weeks. His friend looked tanned and relaxed, as if he'd been on vacation. Owen smiled awkwardly. 'Hey buddy,' he whispered. Rhys nodded happily back.

'Okay, let's get this started. Rhys Sterling. Let's hear it.' Coach pushed Rhys to the front of the stage.

'Two hundred dollars.' Kelsey held up her paddle. Rhys blew a kiss over to her, managing to come off romantic rather than cheesy.

Jack glanced at the stage. Owen looked handsome, but he also looked like he was going to vomit all over the stage.

'Two hundred dollars. What does that include?' Coach leered. 'Okay, so we're going to hold Rhys at two Franklins, and see if anyone wants to match that – for Owen Carlyle?'

Around the elegant event space, tipsy schoolgirls whispered to one another fervently, pooling their money and daring each other to bid.

Jack held up her paddle before anyone else could. 'Two

hundred fifty dollars. For my *boyfriend*,' she added, shooting the general female populace a 'back the fuck off' glare. She glowered at J.P., who was holding Baby's hand in his and examining it like a fucking palm reader.

'Five hundred!' A skinny, goateed guy in the back of the room shot up his hand, waving his paddle wildly.

'Okay, well . . .' Coach looked around the room. A hush had fallen, and the tips of Owen's ears turned bright red.

'So we've got five hundred for Carlyle and two hundred for Sterling . . . Anyone else want Sterling?' Coach looked around the room hopefully.

'Three hundred,' Kelsey cried, bidding over herself. Jack grimaced.

'Okay, so, Sterling for three hundred and Carlyle for five hundred. Going once, going twice . . .' Coach scanned the room one last time, and Jack felt her stomach form a tight knot. She hated how seriously everyone was taking this, as if it were fucking Sotheby's. She'd have to fucking *buy* her fucking imaginary boyfriend with imaginary money.

'Six hundred for Owen.' Jack held up her paddle in the air.

'Sold!' Coach pounded the gavel. Owen's face broke into a wide, relieved grin. He and Rhys hugged each other good-naturedly and walked back to the table to a smattering of applause.

'Thanks, babe.' Owen came back to the table and brushed his lips against Jack's cheek. She felt a weird flutter in her stomach.

'Hey, you're worth it,' Jack teased, even though the thought of paying six hundred dollars was making her a little sick. Onstage, Hugh Moore was being auctioned off. Jack rolled her eyes. They'd made out once, in eighth grade, the first time Jack had ever gotten drunk at a party. She'd had four tequila shots and had ended up with him in his parents' bedroom. They'd been discovered by his buttoned-up society hostess mother, who'd given them a ridiculously unnecessary facts-of-life talk right there – even though all they'd been doing was fully clothed kissing. *Not* something Jack wanted to think about right now.

'Two hundred and fifty dollars!' Jack heard Jiffy's frantic voice ring out through the crowd. Jiffy was practic-ally drooling. *Ugh*. She could have Hugh Moore.

Hugh whooped and snaked down the steps to Jiffy, where they kissed for way longer than was strictly neces-sary, or decent.

'Okay!' Coach stepped back up onto the podium. 'Since all my boys donated themselves to the cause, I figured it wouldn't be fair if I didn't do it too. Let's begin. I'm going to open the bidding at five hundred dollars. And remember, I'm a lonely man who doesn't have a wife to stand up for me.' Coach made puppy dog eyes and Jack sighed, drinking the rest of her drink. Couldn't they get *on* with things? How much longer was this going to take?

And what, exactly, does she have in mind for later?

'Three thousand!' A clarion voice suddenly rang out from one of the parent tables near the back. Even the waiters craned their heads to look. Jack saw Genevieve holding her honey blond head in her hands, shaking it back and forth slowly, as her obviously hammered mom stood up and wavered her way up to the podium. Jack was instantly glad her mother never came to school events.

Only because she never tells her about them.

Coach blushed and quickly buttoned up his shirt. 'Okay, auction's over!' he announced into the microphone. He ceremoniously banged the gavel as the band in the corner started up a merry rendition of 'The Lady Is a Tramp.'

Impeccable timing.

dancing cheek to cheek . . . ish

'So, what's up, buddy?' Rhys leaned over to Owen, who was glaring into his ruby red vodka-spiked Slippery Seal cocktail as if it held the secret to the universe. 'We did pretty good up there.'

'Yeah,' Owen replied shortly. He glanced at Kelsey, engaged in an earnest conversation with Baby. She was animatedly talking with her hands, as if she didn't care who might be watching her. Owen knew she didn't, which was what had always drawn him to her, from the night they'd met. She was beautiful and irreverent and just so *free* . . . and totally convinced he was a soulless asshole. Owen shook his head. He needed to get very, very drunk.

'So, you and Jack seem really good together,' Rhys offered.

'Yeah.' Owen shrugged. He felt like hitting something, or pulling off his tux and diving into the Hudson River.

Hmm . . . the ripping off the tux part sounds intriguing . . .

'Look, dude, are you okay? I know it's been awkward recently, and I'm sorry we haven't been able to hang out more. It's just . . . I've been spending a lot of time with

Kelsey, and, well . . . she'd rather not be around you. I'm sorry, man. I think she thinks you're just a player. I don't really know why, but you know girls. They gossip about everybody and then decide some things are true.' Rhys lowered his voice, hoping he hadn't done the wrong thing by telling Owen how Kelsey really felt. But the thing was, he'd missed hanging out with Owen, and his buddy needed to know the real reason why things had been so weird recently.

'No, it's cool.' Owen pounded the vodka in his flask. He liked the way it burned his throat.

'But we can still hang out,' Rhys said in concern. Owen seemed truly upset. Girls always got so mad when their friends ditched them for their significant others. That must be how Owen felt. He didn't want to be that type of friend.

'Hey, actually, since you are such a ladies' man . . .' Rhys smiled, hoping the praise would pump his buddy up. Just a few weeks ago, Owen had always been there for him. Even when he'd had the ludicrous idea of stalking Kelsey wearing a '70s suit, Owen had been there. 'Listen, I need your advice,' Rhys lowered his voice, but Baby and Kelsey were still deep in conversation, giggling like long-lost best friends.

'Kelsey and I are going to do it tonight,' Rhys confessed. He felt a shiver of excitement run up his spine. He couldn't believe it was finally going to happen. He'd rented out one of the suites upstairs and had everything set up flawlessly. He and Kelsey had even talked about it, so there'd be no surprises tonight: just loving, romantic perfection. He made a mental note *not* to drink any more champagne. He wanted to remember every single moment.

Owen coughed. '*What?*'

Rhys whacked him on the back. 'You okay?'

'I'm fine!' Owen sputtered, backing away as if Rhys had punched him in the gut.

'You sure? I can get Jack to come and administer CPR,' Rhys said, trying to make a joke.

'No!' Owen practically yelled. 'I think I just . . . ah, need some air,' he gasped. He exploded from the stuffy room, his head hammering. Outside of the ballroom, he sat down on a pink love seat and sighed heavily. A security guard eyed him with curiosity.

'Are you okay, sir?'

Owen locked eyes with the security guard and nodded. 'Fine.' *Except my whole fucking life is falling apart.* The guard nodded back and wandered into the ballroom.

Owen pulled himself to a standing position and hurtled toward the heavy oak door on the opposite wall. He wasn't sure where the door led, but he just needed to get *out*.

And into . . . a ladies' room?

Jack sighed as she gazed at her reflection in the plate-glass windows. She was more than dressed for the occasion, in a never-worn mid-thigh brown Chanel dress she'd bought in Paris over the summer and found in the back of her closet, with dainty black Louboutins. But something felt off. Was it her imagination or did her arms seem more slack and rounded than they had been before? She turned to the center of the dance floor and saw Baby and J.P. dancing close together, oblivious to the staggering couples all around them. Her head only reached his shoulder. When J.P. and Jack had danced together, she was always at eye level with him. At warm, chocolate brown eye level. She picked up her half-full drink and took a long sip, hoping to ease the pain of seeing her ex so obviously head over heels.

'Are you okay?' Jack looked up to see Jiffy drunkenly staggering toward her, Hugh in tow. Jack grimaced. She *really* hated when her friends had boyfriends, especially when she didn't. She needed Owen to come back now so at least she wouldn't feel so alone. Where the hell was he, anyway?

She grabbed a small chocolate tart from a silver platter a tuxedoed waiter was holding so she wouldn't have to answer Jiffy's question. She popped it in her mouth and grabbed another one before the waiter left. Fuck it, she might as well just get fat.

'This is *so* much fun!' Jiffy slurred obliviously as she sloppily kissed Hugh. She plunked down in Owen's empty chair, pulling Hugh on top of her. It was amazing how only a few drinks could turn Jiffy into a Girls Gone Wild video. Jack glanced around. Genevieve was sitting in the corner with a flask and her Treo, probably plotting her move to California. She always did that when she felt unappreciated.

Just then, Rhys came over to the table, holding two drinks. 'Hey . . . want one?' He cleared his throat and offered her a glass. She gratefully accepted, sipping carefully so the liquid didn't splash on her dress. She *loved* when guys waited on her. Who cared if it was anti-feminist or whatever? She was a lady, after all.

Just without a Prince Charming.

'Looks like our dates are gone,' Jack realized, peering around the table. 'Wanna go look for them?' She couldn't deal with being surrounded by couples making out anymore.

'Sure,' Rhys agreed. He laced his arm with hers as they strode out of the ballroom.

l-o-v-e

'I heard they're getting engaged.' Jiffy poked Hugh Moore hard.

'Huh?' Hugh looked over from their now empty table in the direction of the dance floor.

Baby sighed and nuzzled into J.P.'s neck. He smelled like a mixture of laundry detergent and leather. It was a good smell, but she found she sometimes missed the random, less staid smells of pot, or the beach.

Or pink cigarettes?

She leaned closer into him. The band had long ago packed up, and right now the DJ was playing a weird Justin Timberlake/Madonna remix. Baby couldn't believe how lame it was, but J.P. really seemed into it. Not like Baby was surprised. He was as mainstream as she was alternative. But, seriously, Justin Timberlake? She could only imagine how much Sydney would make fun of them. Hell, Sydney had made fun of her for even *attending* this party, even though it wasn't like she really had a choice.

'Hey.' She looked up at J.P., who was humming under his breath. Baby smiled, hoping he'd get the hint that she was ready to go.

Somewhere more private?

'Do you want to go find that photographer? It'd be great to have pictures from tonight,' J.P. suggested. Baby nodded, trying to conceal a sigh. She didn't want a picture of this. It all felt so fake. She'd much rather have a picture of the two of them lying on the East Lawn in Central Park, or holding hands as they crossed the Brooklyn Bridge, or just anywhere else. She sighed in frustration.

'You okay?' he asked softly. Baby nodded, even though her feet hurt, her Tatyana Cashman–approved dress felt way too tight, and she was just ready to get *out*. They could go back to her apartment and hang out on the terrace. Just as she was about to suggest it to J.P., he fished into the pocket of his Armani jacket and pulled out a small box. CARTIER was spelled across the top in gold-leaf script. Baby felt a vague sense of panic rising into her throat, the way she felt right before she dove into the icy cold Nantucket ocean. She knew what was about to happen but was in too deep to back out.

'I thought you'd like this.' J.P. smiled shyly as he pushed the box toward her. Wordlessly, she took it out of his hands and removed the lid. Nestled inside the black velvet was a white-gold necklace. The word *love* was spelled out in tiny lowercase letters, each letter hanging pendantlike on the delicate chain.

'It's just something small,' J.P. amended when he saw the distraught expression on her face. The necklace was beautiful, the white gold on each of the tiny letters capturing the ballroom's dim light. It was just something she'd never, *ever* wear. He pulled it out of the box, and she shivered as his hand brushed against her bare neck. She sort of felt like the necklace was choking her, each tiny letter weighing her down.

'Thanks.' She managed a tiny smile. J.P.'s brown eyes were so trusting. They reminded her of the way his dog, Nemo, looked when he really wanted a walk. Suddenly, she was aware that everyone around them was looking at them with curiosity. She *needed* to get out.

'Do you want to do the Barcelona?' she asked urgently. She searched his sharp cheekbones and intelligent brown eyes and thought she saw a flicker of doubt in the way his mouth slightly tightened. Baby sucked in her breath. If he said no, then that was it. But if he said *yes* . . .

'Okay.' J.P. nodded, his face cracking into a wide grin. 'Now?'

'Yeah,' Baby whispered, even though she wanted to scream, *Yes, yes, yes!* For once, J.P. really surprised her, and not for his lamer-than-average taste in music. She looked around but couldn't see Owen or Avery anywhere. She'd just call them later, once they were at the airport. She didn't want J.P. to lose his enthusiasm.

'Let's do it!' Baby exclaimed wildly. J.P. kissed her on the lips and Baby felt a warm rush of gooey romance. Maybe they *were* two of a kind. His eyes were flickering in excitement, and suddenly Baby felt her stomach flip-flop as if she were in a free fall. Once they got to Barcelona, who *knew* what would happen? Baby kissed him, harder and more urgently this time.

'Let's leave now and get our passports,' J.P. whispered as his hands played in her tangled hair. Baby nodded excitedly.

Taxi!

restrooms aren't just for resting

Owen could hear the thumping DJ music in the next room as he leaned against the wall, finally alone for the first time tonight. He looked around. Judging by the lavender scent and pink- and orchid-colored walls, this was definitely the lounge part of a ladies' room. Instead of couches, bathtubs filled with pink and purple pillows were set up around the perimeter of the room.

Owen climbed into one of the tubs and relaxed against the plush pillows. He sighed heavily. Girls had it so easy. They had the best bathrooms, their choice of guys . . . He took a sip from his half-full flask and caught sight of his reflection in the mirror above the tub. He looked wild-eyed and miserable.

Just then, the door opened, and Kelsey wobbled in on four-inch stilettos, as if bidden by some sort of crossed-wire ESP. Owen rubbed his eyes.

'What are you doing in the ladies' room? What, is this how you get girls?' she asked, her voice clipped. Behind her, the door slammed shut ominously. Kelsey's blue eyes were snapping, but she still looked stunningly, achingly beautiful.

'Hey,' Owen replied lamely.

'Why can't you just leave me alone?' Kelsey hissed. 'You know what, I'll just leave.' She sighed heavily and turned abruptly on her heel.

'No, wait!' Owen cried. Kelsey whirled around, her green dress swirling around her tan knees.

'Why? You know I hate you,' she said simply. She bit her lower lip as if she was going to cry. Owen just sat there, feeling like an idiot. He didn't know how he could even begin to tell her how much he loved her, how he'd *never*, *ever* meant to hurt her, how he didn't have a choice. 'What we did together meant *nothing*?' Kat continued angrily. 'What the hell was that? I told you I had never done that before. And then you treated me like this random . . .' She paused, as if searching for the right word. '*Girl!*' she spit out, as if that was the highest insult she could hurl. Owen shook his head helplessly. He hurriedly tried to climb out of the stupid tub, one foot sliding against the slippery marble surface. No matter what, he couldn't let her leave.

'It's not like that,' Owen began. He wished he could run his hands through her hair, or calmly rub her back or . . . something. He thought of Rhys. But suddenly, with Kat in front of him, it was obvious what he had to do.

'Kelsey . . . *Kat* . . . listen, I love you,' he said, his voice cracking. 'It wasn't a one-night thing. I knew I loved you that night, but then I met Rhys and I heard how much *he* loved you, and I couldn't do that to him. I needed to give him a chance.' Why had he ever let her go? Now that he said it, it didn't seem to make any sense at all.

'Yeah, right.' Kelsey shook her head, but her silvery blue eyes seemed uncertain.

'It's true,' Owen said simply. He stepped out of the tub

and over to her. He paused. He wanted to pull her into him. 'I'm so, so, so sorry.'

She stepped closer to him, and all of a sudden, it felt like a current of electricity passed between their bodies. She reached out and pulled his hand against her chest. Owen breathed the achingly familiar scent of the apple shampoo she used. She was perfect. *It* was perfect. He felt her mouth on his and he leaned in, knowing it was wrong. But they would figure that out later. The main thing was, he and Kat were together.

He sat on the edge of one of the pillow-filled bathtubs and pulled her down onto him. He kissed her passionately, urgently. Their hands ran the length of each other's bodies, as if grasping for what they'd both been missing.

'I think this is a ladies' room.'

Owen heard the sound of voices outside the door. Who cared? He continued to kiss Kat hungrily, pulling her down into the tub.

'Oh my God.'

Owen heard a guy's voice. He looked up, gently pushing Kat off of him. Standing frozen by the door were Rhys and Jack.

'Um.' Kelsey scrambled to her feet, slipping and falling back into Owen.

'What the fuck!' Rhys yelled, punching the wall. It made a sickening thud.

'It's not—' Owen and Kat said at the same time, their voices blending together as they scrambled to their feet. Owen looked wildly from Rhys to Jack. He knew this looked bad. Very bad.

'Fuck you,' Jack spat. She looked at Owen, his face red and his hand on Kelsey's back. She'd known he still had feelings for Kelsey, whatever had happened between them in the past. It was so obvious, but to see it, right in front of her fucking face . . . She turned and walked out.

Rhys's hand was throbbing from where he'd punched the wall, and he wanted to cry. But he was driven by the red-hot rage coursing through his veins. He felt like he was going to explode as in one swift movement he took off his Armani jacket and swung, his fist connecting with Owen's face.

'Oh God,' Owen said in surprise as he staggered backward, bright red blood spurting from his nose.

'No!' Kelsey yelled. 'Rhys, what the *fuck*?'

Rhys looked at Kelsey through a film of hot, angry tears. The way she said his name was so harsh, like she truly hated him.

'I'm fine.' Owen shook his head. He covered his nose and eyes with his hand, partly because he couldn't bear to see Rhys's expression.

'Okay, what's going on in here?' Two large bouncers catapulted in angrily at the sound of the commotion. Each one immediately grabbed one of the guys, while Kelsey stood helplessly in the middle.

'It was nothing, sir,' Owen said. Blood gushed onto the pink carpet. 'Just a dare. We're leaving anyway.'

'That true?' The beefy bouncer looked at Rhys suspiciously.

'Yes,' he said woodenly, not meeting Owen's eyes.

'Okay, fine. You kids get out, now.' The bouncer escorted the boys to the elevator, Kelsey trailing behind them.

'I'm sorry,' Owen said dumbly. He couldn't stand the way Rhys looked right now. It would be easier if his face held only pure, unbridled anger, but Owen could tell he was utterly devastated.

'Don't talk to me,' Rhys hissed as the elevator made the agonizingly slow descent down. Finally, they reached the lobby.

Kelsey and Owen hurriedly exited, making their way out of the Delancey and into the oppressive heat. Even though it was late September, the night felt like summer. Like the first time they met.

'Are you okay?' Kelsey asked, her hands fluttering toward Owen's battered nose. Owen nodded. It didn't hurt that badly. What *did* hurt was remembering the look on Rhys's face. Owen closed his eyes to blot out the image and inhaled the vague scent of apples.

'It's nothing, don't worry.' Owen tapped his nose experimentally. To his surprise, it felt fine.

'Do you think – maybe – you should come back to my place to make sure everything's okay?' Kelsey fretted. She looked so sweet and concerned and shy that Owen just wanted to pull her close to him. He glanced up and down the empty street. Suddenly, he realized, he could. They weren't a secret. Kelsey – Kat – was right in front of him. They didn't have to hide.

'Okay,' Owen breathed.

Kelsey's lips spread into a wide grin. Just as quickly, she stopped smiling. 'Promise me we're not bad people?' She looked up pleadingly at him.

Owen shook his head. 'No, we're just . . . meant to be,' he finished lamely. Across the street, a car alarm went off. The past ten minutes had held more emotional drama than he'd been through in his life, and he honestly didn't know what he was supposed to do next.

But Kelsey did.

'Let's go,' she commanded, taking his hand and squeezing it urgently. Owen reacted almost instinctively. He pulled her toward him, not even caring that they were in the middle of the street. Right now, kissing on the corner with blood trickling out of his nose, he actually felt *good*.

Love *is* the best painkiller.

Alone in the elevator, Rhys pressed the up button, hard. Like an idiot, he'd reserved a suite for him and Kelsey for the night. He shook his head numbly. Only when the elevator doors slid closed did more tears fall down his cheek.

He walked into the rose petal–strewn suite and looked out on Manhattan, trying to take it all in. All that time, *Owen* was the other guy? All that time, Owen had taken him for some dumb, trusting sidekick. The joke was on him, but it wasn't funny at all.

Rhys savagely tore the foil around the Veuve chilling in the corner and popped the cork. It ricocheted against the all-white wall, and rivulets of champagne dripped down the orange label of the bottle. They spewed onto the pristine white goose-down bedspread. He laughed bitterly. He had been a fool. Too trusting, too naïve. But that was all going to change.

up, up, and away

The Cashmans' town car dropped Baby off at her building on Seventy-second and Fifth. She ran through the lobby, went up the elevator, and sprinted through their cavernous penthouse. As soon as the door closed, she tore off her dress, letting it fall into a puddle on the buffed floor. Immediately Rothko came over and pawed at it suspiciously. Baby felt a small wave of guilt at the idea of just running off. But she shook it away. She was going to Barcelona!

She ran into her mom's studio, which was currently filled with canvases painted with the number 8 in all different colors, shapes, and sizes. She opened a battered filing cabinet that housed all of the Carlyles' important documents and pulled out her barely used passport. She pulled her hair in a messy bun, threw on a pair of Avery's Citizen jeans, which were about two sizes too big and six inches too long, and yanked on an ancient navy blue hoodie that said SNUG HARBOR with a picture of a smiling whale on the back. She stuffed her wallet, a copy of *The Unbearable Lightness of Being*, and a sketch book in an army green messenger bag that looked perfect for an adventure, then tore down the elevator and through the doors again.

'Can I get you a cab, miss?' the doorman asked, tipping his hat.

Baby nodded eagerly. She couldn't believe she'd be somewhere totally different in less than twelve hours. Suddenly, she shivered despite the surprisingly balmy late-September air. Should she have brought a coat? What was the weather in Barcelona like, anyway? Who *cared*? She could always buy a coat.

Or snuggle with J.P.?

Just as she slammed the yellow door of the cab, her phone beeped. She slid it out of her front pocket. *Meet at 12th Ave. and 48th St x J.P.* Weird. Why were they going all the way over to the West Side? Maybe that was a shortcut to get to Kennedy or wherever.

As the cab zoomed crosstown through the ghostly-looking park, Baby wondered if she should feel guilty. After all, she wasn't *officially* done with her Constance community service, and she and Sydney were supposed to figure out the layout for the *Rancor* fashion shoot, not to mention round up all the clothing samples they'd borrowed. But Baby quickly brushed those thoughts aside as the cab careened southwest. She hadn't felt this excited in a long time. Maybe she could use *this* experience for another *Rancor* essay – teaching Constance girls to live outside their navy uniform–wearing, sesame crusted tuna–eating, vodka gimlet–swilling lives.

'Here we are.' The cabbie stopped at a parking lot adjacent to the Hudson River.

'Okay.' Baby slid out of the cab and handed the driver a twenty. *Where should I go, exactly?* she texted. Just then, her phone rang.

'Are you here?' J.P. asked excitedly.

Baby looked around. 'Yeah, but all I see are helicopters and stuff.'

'Okay, well, we're right on Forty-ninth Street – there's a path, just walk right up.'

'Oh.' Baby looked up and couldn't believe she hadn't noticed the gold glint of the interlocking *C*'s on a white helicopter. She quickly walked over, her hands shoved in her pockets.

'There you are!' J.P. wrapped his arms around her in a bear hug. 'I told my dad – he's so psyched for us. He's arranging details with our pilot, so we should get there by tomorrow morning, around eleven their time, and I've booked us at the Ritz.' J.P.'s face shone with excitement.

A private jet? The Ritz? Baby kicked a small pebble on the tarmac in frustration. It all sounded perfect – for a girl like Avery or Jack. For Baby, it was entirely wrong. She didn't *want* a five-star hotel or a private plane. The point was to get out of New York City and experience *the world* – not the exact same thing in a different country. J.P. was still dressed up in his suit from tonight, and he looked achingly handsome, his brow furrowed in concern. Baby bit her lip numbly. He just didn't get it.

'We'll definitely be able to get back by Monday. Or we could both just take a sick day from school or something,' J.P. explained, letting the sentence hang in the air. Baby managed a small smile. She couldn't believe J.P. thought she was worried about school. He was *such* a good guy. She felt like the worst person in the world for what she was going to do.

'I don't . . . I don't think this is going to work.' Baby looked at the ground, noticing the ultra-buffed shoes of the pilot, who was standing five feet away, pretending not to listen.

'It's just . . . we're too different,' Baby explained. 'You want to fly in jets, and I just want to fly.' Baby smiled, remembering the day they'd met. J.P. had hired her to manage his out-of-control puppies after one ran off and she chased it barefoot down the street. 'You need someone who appreciates how amazing you are.'

'I think *you're* amazing,' J.P. said.

'You too,' Baby replied genuinely. It was really true. She bit her lip, then continued in a rush of words. 'You introduced me to the city. You showed me it could be fun. Now I need to find that for myself.' She shrugged and smiled sadly up at him. It was weird. Their breakup felt so natural. And, judging from J.P.'s wistful but resigned expression, it seemed he felt the same way. She couldn't believe she was giving up a guy any other girl in Manhattan would *kill* for. And she couldn't believe the bubbling sense of freedom she felt in her stomach.

'Can I at least get you a cab, Ms Independent?' J.P. teased good-naturedly.

'That'd be nice,' Baby acquiesced. It was nice to be taken care of sometimes. J.P. hailed her a cab and they hugged tenderly. 'Call me if you need your dogs walked?' Baby asked impishly. A tear fell out of her eye and she laughed halfheartedly. She didn't know why it hurt so much. It was like when she'd visited her home in Nantucket and found it didn't feel the same. J.P. brushed the tear aside as a cab screeched to a halt.

'Friends?' J.P. pulled her in close and kissed the top of her head.

'Always.' Baby gave him a genuine smile as she reached

around her neck and unclasped the LOVE necklace. 'Thank you.'

J.P. nodded and held the door of the cab open for her. Baby stepped in, squeezing his hand one last time.

The door slammed shut and Baby eased into the backseat. The dreadlocked cabbie turned down the reggae music blasting from the speakers. He peered at Baby, her passport still clutched in her tiny hand.

'The airport, miss?' he asked, staring pointedly at the passport.

Baby looked out the cab window. It had started to rain, and the tiny drops pelting the glass made everything look extra sparkly. Just a matter of yards away was the fast-moving Hudson. Even though she knew the land on the other side was just New Jersey, from here it looked beautiful and mysterious and full of surprises. And she needed a little bit of surprise. She caught the eye of the cabbie and nodded, a tiny smile playing on her lips.

Bon voyage?

boys aren't everything

Avery woke up, sober and alone, in her bedroom on Sunday morning. She glanced at the clock on her dresser. Eleven a.m. In another, allergen-free universe, she'd be showering and getting ready for a romantic brunch, followed by a stroll through the Met with Tristan. But unfortunately, in her dysfunctional world, she really didn't have to wake up for anything. She sighed and pulled her pillow over her head, determined to shut out the world for as long as possible.

Just then, her phone rang on her bedside table

'Hello?' she asked flatly. She couldn't imagine who it could be. Maybe she should just cut her losses and become a feminist, adopt fifty cats, and write difficult-to-understand treatises on the male gaze.

'Avery, darling, I do hope it's not too early to call,' the crackly voice of Muffy St Clair came through the receiver.

'Not at all.' Avery sat up, suppressing a sigh, and pushed her hair behind her ears.

'Well, I'm meeting a few of the ladies at L'Absinthe for brunch and I think one in particular would be *quite* interested in meeting you,' Muffy croaked. She sounded as if she'd just smoked a pack of Merits. Maybe she had.

'Oh.' Avery tried to fake enthusiasm. She couldn't wait to spend her Sunday afternoon talking about the cafeteria complaint box at Constance or something equally riveting.

'Fantastic! Noon okay for you, dear?' Muffy hung up quickly, not giving her much of a choice. But at least she hadn't asked about the benefit last night, so Avery didn't have to lie about Muffy's sneezy mess of a grandson. Avery rolled out of bed and, not bothering to shower, pulled on a simple lilac-colored Tory Burch sheath dress. She wondered if Baby had bothered to come home last night, or if she'd ended up spending the night with J.P. Not like she was jealous or anything.

Not at all.

''Bye!' Avery yelled in the foyer just in case *anyone* in her family had bothered to come home. Hearing no response, she grabbed her Louis Vuitton Speedy purse and slammed the door extra loudly on the way out. She was *so* not in the mood. She took the elevator downstairs and ran into a bleary-eyed Owen in the lobby. A black and blue bruise was spreading from under his nose to the area under his eyes. What the hell?

'Oh my God! Did Jack do that?' Avery asked indignantly. His whole face looked swollen and painful.

'No.' Owen shook his head. 'Long story. Long, involved story,' he said mysteriously. 'With a sort-of-happy ending.' Instantly, the expression on his face changed from one of misery to one of happiness. But another wave of emotion passed over him, and the expression shifted to one of regret. Avery regarded him with curiosity.

And they think girls are hard to understand?

'Are you *okay*?' she asked again. Why was Owen being so weird? 'And where were you last night? Are you just getting home?'

'Long story,' Owen repeated, his voice muffled from the injury. Avery glanced at her Rolex, torn. She wanted to hear what the black eye was all about, but she was already running late.

'Look, I'll tell you all about it later. I need to clean up more before I see Mom,' he explained.

'Okay, but we're going to have a conversation. I have to go to a brunch now, but three o'clock, we're talking. Be there,' Avery commanded.

She walked outside and made her way down Fifth, toward Sixty-seventh Street. She entered the café, looking for her familiar crew of platinum blond ladies.

'Avery!' she heard a thin voice call. The gnarled hand of Muffy St Clair gestured her over to a corner table. She faked her best smile and walked over to them.

'Avery, darling.' Muffy stood up and kissed her on both cheeks. Avery fought the urge to rub off the lipstick stains she was sure Muffy left in her wake. Her gaze fell on the tiny woman sitting at the table. She wore six Chanel chain belts over an Yves Saint Laurent black dress, her henna-dyed red hair teased a full six inches above her widow's peak. 'This is Ticky Bensimmon-Heart,' Muffy made the introduction. 'I was telling her about you, and she so wanted to see you in person.'

'So far, not too disappointing.' Ticky nodded her head approvingly as she downed her mimosa. Avery felt her heart skip a beat. Ticky Bensimmon-Heart, editor in chief of *Metropolitan*, was impressed by her!

'Good to meet you!' Avery stuck out her hand, hoping she didn't sound too eager.

'Sit,' Ticky commanded, gesturing to an empty chair. Impatiently, she waved a hovering waiter away. 'I make it a point not to eat during the day,' Ticky explained.

'Tickyrexia,' Muffy clarified for Avery's benefit. 'She's been doing it since, when, the Kennedy inauguration? But, darling, we want to hear about *you*. And Tristan?' Muffy sat back expectantly as she drained her own mimosa.

'Well . . .' Avery paused, looking at the two women. Should she lie?

'You bitch.' Ticky laughed a loud, throaty laugh, shaking her head at Muffy. Muffy threw her head back and joined in.

'Um, he was very . . .' Avery began desperately.

'Let me guess? Tristan had one of his spells. Classic!' Ticky chuckled. 'Muffy, why'd you do that to our girl?'

Muffy laughed ruefully. Curious patrons turned to stare.

'I'm so sorry,' she said, wiping a tear of laughter from her crinkly under-eye. 'I thought he was growing out of it.'

'You *knew*?' Avery asked sharply. *That you set me up with Mr Walking Allergen?* she wanted to add. Instead, she took a long sip of water. Did *everyone* just want to see her get in the most ludicrous situations possible? She considered what would happen if she just walked out of the restaurant, away from Muffy and from the entire humiliating SLBO position. Let Constance get ugly midnight blue uniforms. She was *so done*.

'Oh, darling, I didn't mean any harm.' Muffy took note of Avery's darkening expression. 'Really, I did you a favor.

I couldn't very well let you go out with Esther's grandson. He's a terrible prick.' Muffy shrugged and then cackled again. She and Ticky laughed together, sounding sort of like the witches from *Macbeth*.

Double, double, old ladies are trouble.

'Well, I need to head off,' Avery said crisply, trying to sound polite. She had *much* better things to do than be made fun of by drunk senior citizens.

'Don't leave us!' Ticky exclaimed, obviously disappointed. 'Consider it your initiation. And you're quite a pistol – cheers to that!' She lifted her mimosa glass and smiled. 'How'd you like to intern for me at *Metropolitan*?'

Avery glanced at her. *Really? Metropolitan* was the coolest, most sophisticated magazine. Internships were absurdly hard to get. Was Ticky serious?

'You'll start Monday,' Ticky commanded. Avery looked from one woman to the other. She'd totally hug them right now, if she didn't think she would break them. Instead, she motioned for the waiter. It was time to celebrate.

what goes around comes around

Jack walked down Fifth on Sunday morning. She didn't have a clear destination; she just wanted to walk and think. She still felt stung over what had happened last night, even though it wasn't as if Owen had ever been her *real* boyfriend. She hugged her arms around her chest. The weather was getting colder, and she suddenly felt very alone.

She paused in front of the Cashman Complexes, looking at the gilt *C*'s. It was as if she'd been pulled there. She felt a knot in her stomach. She really missed the way things used to be.

'Hey beautiful.' J.P.'s voice surprised her, and she whipped around. He always used to greet her that way. And *she* always used to dress up before she saw him. Today she wore an old pair of black Citizen skinny jeans, Miu Miu gray suede boots, and an ancient, oversize Theory sweater and had on no makeup. But she didn't really care.

'You don't have to say that,' Jack said shortly. 'I was just walking by,' she added lamely, so she didn't seem like a total stalker.

'It's good to see you,' J.P. said. One of his puggles was curiously sniffing her ankle. She'd always thought his dogs were gross, but this one seemed kind of cute. At least it was friendly. She bent down and gingerly patted its furry dark head.

'Anyway, I'm just walking the dogs,' J.P. stated, as if it weren't obvious.

'Okay.' Jack backed away. A week ago, she would have wanted to kick J.P., hard. Now, with his hands balled into the pockets of his dorky khakis, he didn't look like the evil life-wrecker she'd imagined.

'Want to come with me?' J.P. blurted. He blushed.

Jack regarded him suspiciously. 'Why? Where's your girlfriend?' Jack cringed as the words left her lips. But she couldn't help it. Her life sucked, his didn't. She'd been cheated on and dumped by an *imaginary* boyfriend. It really didn't get any worse than that, not even on that stupid French drama her mom was going to star in.

'She dumped me. What about your boyfriend?' J.P. countered.

'Didn't work out.' She shrugged, trying not to smile. Baby Carlyle had dumped J.P.? There was a twist she hadn't seen coming. 'Here, give me a leash,' she commanded, grabbing the Louis Vuitton leash attached to the smallest, least gross puggle. She quickly strode into the park. The air smelled like fall: honey-roasted peanuts and leaves. Things were changing.

'By the way, I heard about what happened with your dad . . . Why didn't you tell me?' J.P. touched Jack's arm. She felt a jolt of electricity run up and down her body, and looked into his friendly brown eyes.

'I just . . . It was just so fucked up.' Jack sighed angrily. 'I just can't deal with other people's shit, you know?' She didn't mean to sound so hysterical, but she did. A little bit. She took a deep breath and shrugged. 'It doesn't matter anymore.'

'Yes, it does,' J.P. chided. 'You should have told me.'

Together, they walked through the winding path of the park, which was crowded with dog walkers, runners, and families enjoying the crisp early-fall air. 'I missed you, Jack,' J.P. said simply. Jack nodded. She *hated* sappy conversations. Without another word, she turned to J.P. and kissed him. He tasted the same, like cough drops. Nemo barked appreciatively.

Everything in Jack's body melted. After all the pain and grief, all the conniving and blackmailing, she'd gotten what she wanted. She kissed J.P. eagerly, waiting for that familiar click – *perfection* – the moment when she'd know everything was exactly as it used to be.

But as they pulled apart, Jack felt her eyes instinctively drawn east, toward a certain Fifth Avenue penthouse. She couldn't help but wonder what Owen was doing, or who he was with.

The more things stay the same, the more they change.

gossipgirl.net
Disclaimer: All the real names of places, people, and events have been altered or abbreviated to protect the innocent. Namely, me.

| topics | sightings | your e-mail | post a question |

hey people!

good morning, party people!

First, a poll: how many of you actually slept in your bed last night? And if you did, how many of you slept *alone*? Let's see a show of hands! For those of you who took part in the St Jude's swim team bidding – charity aside – was it worth it?

And now, for those who are too hungover to do anything other than consume the cinnamon raisin toast and black currant tea your housekeeper oh so thoughtfully brought you, here's the news you've missed:

is the bromance over?

Running on the river, long, lingering conversations over fries at 3 Guys, sharing drinks in Sheep Meadow . . . Angelina and Brad? Not quite. It used to be our favorite pair of swim team buddies. Now, however, it seems like there's more than bad blood between **R** and **O** – there's a bloody nose. Luckily, **K** seems to be an excellent nurse. And not for the friend you'd think! She and **O** were spotted just this morning at a diner on Second, having a cozy brunch. As for **R**, he's had to console himself with an ultra-exclusive suite at the Delancey and a bottle of Veuve. I guess all good things do have to come to an end, but I'll admit it: I'm sad about this one!

power breakfast

Move over, Michael's. Seems like L'Absinthe is the new place for media power confabs, at least judging from this morning, where **A** was having a very serious discussion with none other than Ticky Bensimmon-Heart. Luckily, no one was sneezing. Next up for **A**: a foray into the cutthroat world of magazines? She's certainly got the pluck for it . . . and we all know ambition is the most important accessory.

sundays in the park

Seems like there was more than puppy love in Central Park this morning. **J** and **J.P.** appear to be back together, and, according to passersby, better than ever. Does the reunion of the king and queen of the Upper East Side mean that **J**'s spell of bad luck has been broken? Well, I'll throw another iron in the fire: after a long deliberation process, the School of American Ballet is apparently set to announce its scholarship recipients today, which could either signal the beginning of the end for **J**, or the makings of a serious comeback. Long live the queen?

last seen leaving

The whimsically romantic **B**, spotted in a standby line at JFK. Holding a toothbrush and passport, wearing her sister's castoffs . . . and a big smile. Where to? Also, a certain Spanish party boy last seen clubbing in Barcelona. Probably a coincidence.

So, you ask, what does this all mean? It means that I'll be keeping very close tabs on everyone and everything. Why? Because someone has to. Life changes in an instant. Just like you depend on your MAC lip gloss, your venti half-caf skim cap, and your BlackBerry Pearl to get you through even the toughest

days, you can depend on me to tell you what you need to hear.
Promise.

You know you love me

Gossip Girl

Can't wait for your next fix of
scandal and intrigue?

**Visit www.thegossipgirl.co.uk for
regular GOSSIP GIRL updates.**

Download great extras and free content

Submit your reviews and recommendations

Win fantastic prizes in our
regular competitions

And so much more!

We'd love to know what you think about
GOSSIP GIRL THE CARLYLES.
Email us at gossipgirl@headline.co.uk

Every girl dreams about it. Some just have it. How far would you go to become THE IT GIRL?

Enter the world of the über-rich, super-glam and totally cool. These girls wear the best clothes, date the best guys, whisper the best secrets and have the *worst* behaviour. High fashion, hot guys and delicious gossip . . . what more could a girl want?

Jenny Humphrey left Constance Billard in less than ideal circumstances – apparently she was a bad influence on the other girls . . . But leaving the up-tight Manhattan all-girls school doesn't seem like such a bad thing when you've been accepted at Waverly Academy – the elite boarding school where glamorous rich kids don't let the rules get in the way of an excellent time.

Now she's determined to shed her crazy city past by reinventing herself. Goodbye Old Jenny – hello ultra-sophisticated New Jenny.

From the author of the massively popular GOSSIP GIRL books, an addictive new series.

THE IT GIRL
NOTORIOUS
RECKLESS
UNFORGETTABLE
LUCKY